THE DEMON'S BARGAIN

A PECULIAR TASTES NOVEL

KATEE ROBERT

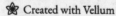

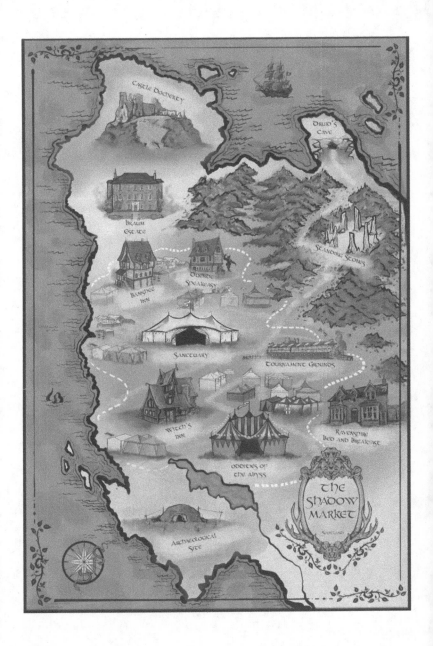

CONTENT NOTES

Please be aware that some content in this book may be triggering for some readers. Reader discretion is advised.

TROPES: Demon deals, forced proximity

TAGS: Enby demon, murderous witch, demon deals, forced proximity, only one bed, magical pegging, beheading as a love language, all my exes are in love and I'm sad, sexy but sweet, Chekov's lube

CONTENT WARNINGS: Some incidental injuries during sex, murder, blood-related magic, explicit sex

CHAPTER 1

LENORA

I can't believe it's come to this.

My knees hurt from kneeling on the basement floor as I painstakingly draw the summoning circle. I keep pausing to reference my great-grandmother's grimoire. I had to sneak it out of the house during the last family dinner; neither of my fathers would be pleased that I'm following in *her* footsteps.

Desperate times call for desperate measures.

If I told them what'd I'd done, that I let my foolish heart lower my defenses with the wrong person and lost the family amulet as a result... They wouldn't yell at me. They certainly wouldn't throw things or have a messy reaction. They'd just be disappointed, which is worse in so many ways.

No, I have to do this on my own.

The amulet has some of the most powerful protective spells in existence laced into it. When someone wears it, they can't be poisoned or attacked by magical means—or at least magical means from *this* realm.

I'm betting everything that a bargainer demon will have the firepower to retrieve it. If they kill Kristoff in the process?

All the better. I don't *think* he's had it long enough to learn it's secret, but every day that passes raises the risk.

I shudder and quickly finish the runes around the circle. "There." I stand slowly and check the circle on the ground against the one drawn in the grimoire. According to the book, each bargainer demon has their own calling card, so to speak. This one will call Ramanu, a bargainer demon with gargoyle blood in their lineage. I'm not sure if that makes a difference when it comes to getting what I want, but it was noted here, so maybe it's worth noting.

Then again, the book also goes into rather explicit detail about the demon. They didn't fuck my great-grandmother, but based on this, she absolutely would have been down for it. It's enough to wonder what my father thought when he read through this grimoire. I laugh softly. Ultimately, she didn't make a deal, though she summoned Ramanu three separate times.

Probably trying to get in their pants.

That's not on the agenda for me—even if it were, the bargainer demons' terms are too strict. Seven years' service for whatever task they agree to. Too long. The cost is too high.

But losing my power...being responsible for *my family* losing its power?

Yeah, talk about desperate times.

I crouch and stare at the circle. I could try to get the amulet again on my own. I don't have to track Kristoff across the world. The bastard travels more than a flight attendant but with much less predictability—yet he won't for the next three days.

It's Samhain.

He'll be at the Shadow Market, along with everyone else worth knowing in this realm. Even some from beyond it. Samhain is one of those special times when the veils thin and shit goes a bit weird. Normally, I adore it. I spend the three days at the market visiting with friends, stocking up on magical items that only seem to be available this time of year, and finding a gorgeous partner or four to fuck away the nights with.

Not this time.

I hesitate. If I could do this on my own, I would have managed it by now. Kristoff has had the amulet for two weeks. I haven't seen my powers dampen yet, but it's only a matter of time. My fathers live a mostly quiet life, but what if there's an exception to that rule in the near future and Dad reaches for his magic to protect himself...and nothing answers?

No, I'm out of time and out of options.

With a muttered curse, I grab my dagger and slice along my forearm. Not a deep cut. Just enough to activate the summoning spell written in the grimoire. I speak slowly, carefully, each word layering upon the one before it and making the air in the room spark and sizzle. It's uncomfortable, and my arm is bleeding too freely, the magic in my blood fueling the spell. The circle closes with a snap that vibrates through the room and sends me tipping back onto my ass.

I curse again. "Godsdamned demons and their godsdamned circles." Not that I have much experience with summoning circles, but it worked for my great-grandmother three separate times. If Ramanu is still among the living, it will summon them.

The circle flares purple and then red, the center going strangely fluid. It parts like water, four horns appearing, followed by a head and shoulders. They're exactly as described. One set of horns curls out from their temples and another angles back from their eye sockets, following the curve of their shaved skull.

I can even see what attracted her to them. They're rather good-looking in a demonic sort of way, with high cheekbones and a sensual mouth that curves as I stare. They heft themself from the magical hole in the floor and place their feet on the now-solid ground. Gods, they're tall. My basement ceiling is seven feet high, and their horns scrape across the surface as they look around; they don't have eyes, but they're obviously using magic to examine the area.

I take the opportunity to study them. No matter what the various churches believe, bargainer demons aren't scouring the earth in search of human souls. Honestly, I don't know of a single person who's actually dealt with them personally. But there are rumors.

There are always rumors.

I'm not sure what I expect, but Ramanu finishes their examination and focuses on me. "Hello, little witch."

"Demon." I study them right back. Gods, they cut a fine figure. Broad shoulders. Long black claws that match their horns. Deep crimson skin and teeth that are little too sharp. They're wearing loose, flowing black pants and a fitted black shirt. It's not quite a Catholic priest's getup, but it's close enough. "You look like something out of a naughty nun's wet dream. Did you dress up just for me?"

They laugh, a deep, booming sound. "A summoning is rare. I like to look the part."

"The part of a demonic priest?"

"Not quite." They touch their collar. It's round and fitted, but there isn't a bit of white in sight. "You're not terrified at all. That's a relief. Dealing with the sobbing and hysterics is exhausting."

I might be desperate, but I'm not *that* desperate. I glare. "You're the one in my circle. Maybe you should be terrified of *me*."

If anything, their smile broadens, flashing those too-sharp teeth. "All right, little witch. I'll play. Show me your claws."

I tighten my grip on the dagger. A laughable impulse. Their claws might not be as long as my blade, but the demon has a longer reach than I do. They could rip me to shreds before mustered the proper words for a spell to send them back to the demon realm.

Or they'd be able to if they weren't trapped in the circle.

I purposefully turn my back to them and walk to the table where I arranged all the things I need for this spell. The bandages are ready and waiting for me, so I quickly wrap up the cut on my arm. Without the magic pulling blood from me, it's already started to clot.

Once that's done, I face the demon and lean against the table. Their smile is still firmly in place, and I get the feeling that I've amused them. Lovely. It's going to be quite the challenge to come out of this on top, but I'll do my damnedest. "I have no interest in showing you my claws, Ramanu." Their name shivers across my tongue. Best not examine *that* too closely. "That's not why I called you here."

"Pity." They slide their hands into their pockets. "Very well. Let's hear your opening offer."

It's tempting to continue circling, but we both know I called them here for a reason. Time is of the essence. "There's a witch who took something from me."

"You want it back."

"Yes." I nod slowly. "But, equally important, I want him dead."

They don't have brows to raise, but I get the impression all the same. "Bloodthirsty."

"Practical. It's become a contest of who's better. If I get it back, he'll take it personally, and I'm not interested in looking over my shoulder for the rest of my life." A believable enough story, but the truth is more complicated. If Kristoff realizes the amulet has enough power to boost the magic of an entire bloodline, he'll never stop trying to get it back.

"I see." They cock their head to the side. "Very well. I'll kill this witch for you—"

"No."

"No?"

It would be simpler—smarter—to allow Ramanu to take care of the problem. Kristoff might be a force to be reckoned with, and I'm nearly certain one of his parents is paranormal rather than human, but he's no match for a *demon.*

But... "That motherfucker stole from me. I want to be the one to end him, and I want to see the light dying in his eyes when he realizes it's me who's responsible."

"Seven years."

I blink. "Excuse me?"

"I will happily do as you ask, but it will require seven years in payment." They hold their finger up when I start to argue. "Those are standard terms, which I'm sure you're aware of if you had enough information to summon me in the first place."

They *were* standard terms according to the grimoire. I cross my arms over my chest. "I was under the impression that the bargainer demons have new management." Great-Grandmother had a note in the margins about that and her hopes that it would affect how bargains were made. She died before she was able to summon Ramanu a fourth time to test it out. "Why are the deals the same?"

Ramanu laughs softly and paces the circle. "They aren't the same, little witch. Azazel's values are not... Well, best not to say *her* name. The humans who take contracts with us are significantly better treated than they were previously."

So they say. "Forgive me if I'm not comforted. Seven years is too long. I'll give you one." A year away from my life is almost too much to bear, but it's worth it to accomplish this. I don't have another choice.

They snort. "We are *bargainer* demons. Not hagglers. Seven years is the cost. Take it or leave it." Ramanu tilts their head to the side as if hearing something I can't. "There are plenty of humans who will play with me. Stop wasting both our time."

Frustration wells up inside me, weeks' worth of fear and desperation morphing to fury in a single instant. "Impossible to make those deals when you're trapped in *my* circle."

They laugh.

It's the only warning I get before they flick the air over the top of the drawn circle with a single finger. It shatters. There's no sound that ears can hear, but the backlash hits me hard enough to knock me back a few steps. A blink and they're in front of me, bracketing me in with their big arms and leaning close. "Who's trapped now, little witch?"

I react on instinct, slamming my hands to their chest and snarling, "*Back*."

They fly back several feet, skidding across the concrete floor. "Someone truly does have claws of her own." They grin. "I like it."

"Touch me without permission and I'll gut you."

Ramanu straightens and flicks some dust off their shirt. "I'm not interested in those kinds of games, Lenora." They must see me jolt because they shake their head. "Come now. You must know we've been watching you. So increasingly desperate to get back that little trinket. You're ripe for the picking."

This is a waste of time. I won't leave behind my life for seven years, and they obviously won't budge on the terms. It makes sense in a fucked-up kind of way. Magic can be a fickle beast, so it likes rules. The more people who believe the rule, the more powerful the magic it can summon. Seven is a number with significance in more cultures than I care to count off the top of my head. "Enough of this. I'm done. I'll find another way."

I'm in the process of turning away when their voice stops me cold. "Normally we prefer payment up front, but I'm willing to massage the rules for you." A pointed pause. "And the time that passes in the human world during those years will be negligible."

I know better than to engage with this, but knowing better doesn't stop me from eyeing them. "How negligible?"

"It's not a strict ratio, but at best guess, you'll be gone a few hours to a few weeks. A month at most."

There are plenty of theories that time moves differently in the various realms, but I hadn't realized *how* differently. "I'm not sure I feel like answering questions on why I've aged seven years in a few days."

They sigh. "You're being intentionally difficult. A side effect of the magic saturation that causes the time difference is that people in my realm age slower. As I said, it's not an exact science, but you'll be just as young and beautiful as you are now." Again, they appraise me in a way that makes my body go tight.

I have a varied history of partners, but the truth is danger is my favorite aphrodisiac. It's why I keep choosing people like Kristoff, who are bad for me. Things are hot and sexy right up until they go sideways, and they *always* go sideways. Letting desire override my common sense is what got me into this mess to begin with.

Ramanu does that strange listening thing again. As far as I'm aware of, bargainer demons don't have much in the way of telepathy, but most of my information is from my grimoire, and my great-grandmother had other priorities that weren't fully categorizing them as a people. She was only interested in Ramanu. It's entirely possible bargainers have more powers than I can begin to guess at. "A counterproposal."

"You're countering your own proposal."

They shrug. "You're attending the Shadow Market."

I consider denying it, but ultimately it's not a secret. "And?"

"I'll attend with you. The bargain is on the table for the duration."

I narrow my eyes. "What's your deal, Ramanu?" Their name feels strange on my tongue...*good*. I give myself a mental shake. I can*not* afford to let desire cloud my judgment. Not again. "Why are you so invested in me taking this bargain? As you said, there are plenty of other desperate humans who would jump at the chance."

"Wait and see, little witch. Wait and see."

CHAPTER 2

RAMANU

I like this little witch.

Lenora.

Her magic bites the air with her frustration and anger. She does a good job of keeping it locked down, but I'm particularly sensitive to this sort of thing thanks to my gargoyle parent. I like the feel of it against my skin. I might not be able to see in the strictest sense of the word, but my magic gives off energy that paints a picture all the same. Lenora's magic twists against mine, little flickers of sensation that make my skin prickle. It makes me want to take a bite out of her.

I can practically hear Azazel's smooth voice in my ear, snarling at me to close the deal. He's much kinder than our last leader, but that's not saying much. We bargainer demons are all about the result, and the result is that our very power comes from engaging in bargains. Azazel is invested in all our people increasing their power, even as he works to maximize the overall power of our territory in our realm.

It's not often we can engage in a bargain with a magical human. They tend to solve their own problems. Lenora agreeing to my bargain would be a significant boost—one I'll need if I'm required to continue babysitting the humans Azazel sent with the other territory leaders as part of the master plan he refuses to explain.

The dragon's bride alone seems to want me dead, because she keeps using me to taunt her husband.

It's amusing, so I allow it, but it would be helpful if I weren't worried about him ripping out my throat when I take my jokes too far. With Lenora's bargain, I would get a magical boost that would put me nearly on Sol's level. Even the playing field, so to speak. I have no interest in the bride—nor she in me—but I'm partial to living.

Plus, the timing of this couldn't be more perfect. I've never had cause to attend the Shadow Market. It's legendary even in our realm, a holdover from a time when our people and the human realm mingled more freely. Some of my people manage to time it right and attend every year, but I've never quite managed it.

Lenora paces in front of me, her energy disturbing the room. It makes the space flicker and fade in my mind's eye, but it's fine. I mapped this room the moment I arrived. We're in a basement of some sort. Concrete is a great damp-ener of magic, unless it's mixed specially to work in a different way, so it makes sense that she'd come here to summon me.

"Stop tracking my movement. You're distracting me."

I'm staring right where her energy flares. I get a glimpse of large eyes, full lips, and hair that flicks around her in a wind neither of us can feel. She's damn powerful. It's what drew me to her in the first place. That and her desperation. It's like a beacon for my people. If she hadn't summoned me, then I would have approached her within a week. "You're distracted by little old me? I'm flattered."

Lenora presses her full lips together and shakes her head. "No. I'm not flirting with you, and I'm not taking you with me to the Shadow Market." I can tell she's trying to say it firmly, but there's an edge to her voice.

I might have been the one caught looking, but she's looking right back.

I lean down until our faces are nearly even. Every time her energy flares, I get a flash of her features, her magic licking across her skin. Pretty thing, isn't she? At least as far as humans are concerned. Like most of my people, I have varied tastes when it comes to bedroom partners. Humans, bargainer demons, the rare paranormal person from the human realm. Even a succubus or incubus on the occasion I feel like pulling Rusalka's tail by fucking one of her people.

It's generally taboo to fuck a human in the midst of making a bargain. After? Well, that's a different story, depending on the demon and human involved. But Azazel is a stickler for the rules, and bargains must be entered into without any kind of coercion.

Our fearless leader is a stick-in-the-mud, but he's fucking terrifying when he's crossed. As a result, I only do it occasionally to keep him on his toes. I'm perverse by nature, and I can't help that I enjoy poking at the people around me.

Lenora is pretty enough to be worth weathering Azazel's wrath.

This is a careful balance. She seems the type to dig in her heels out of principle if I push too hard. Cutting off her nose to spite her face and all that. Unfortunately for her, I'm just as stubborn.

And I have an ace up my sleeve. "Suit yourself, little witch. Be sure to tell me how the next dinner with your fathers goes when they realize you've lost the family heirloom."

Her magic shivers, shifting from purple and red to a horror-struck light gray. "Fuck you."

"Only if you ask nicely."

She sputters, but the colors shift again, anger once more taking hold. "Fine, demon. You can come with me to the Shadow Market—but only so I can make you someone else's problem. I'm *not* giving you seven years. I'll take care of Kristoff myself."

She'll try.

She's powerful enough that if he were anyone else, she'd likely manage it. Kristoff Nilsen is on another level entirely. The Nilsen family has been reproducing with a very specific blend of paranormal for generations. I can't divine out all the threads, but there's vampire, shifter, and even the tiniest thread of seraphim from back when *they* were still present in the human realm.

It's no wonder Lenora hasn't managed to pull off reclaiming her trinket. His home is triple warded, and he travels with more protection than some world leaders. I know. I checked.

"But let's get one thing straight, Ramanu." She reaches out and trails a single finger down the center of my chest. My body tightens in response, and I can't help leaning forward. Just a little.

I like the way she says my name.

Lenora's other hand snaps out and wraps around one of my horns, jerking my head down until our noses nearly touch. Her magic washes over me, the red of anger edging into a nearly neon pink of lust. Oh yes, my little witch isn't unaffected at all. She yanks on my horn again, wrenching my head sideways. "If you fuck with me, I *will* kill you."

"You'll try. It will be fun."

"You—"

I move before she has a chance to finish her sentence, straightening until I nearly take her off her feet by grabbing her around the waist. "Let me make myself perfectly clear, Lenora." She snarls, but I ignore it, walking us to the table and setting her on it. "If you touch me again, I'm going to take it as an invitation."

"I just *attacked* you."

"Baby, that's practically foreplay."

The pink in her magic flares brighter, eating away at the edges of the red. "I'm not going to fuck you."

"Keep telling yourself that." It might be taboo to mix sex with bargaining before a contract is signed, but afterward it's fair game if both parties are consenting. She just ensured that I'm not leaving the human realm without her at my side.

I mean to have Lenora, body and soul.

CHAPTER 3

LENORA

I know better than to fuck a demon.

Truly, I do.

I'm just having a hard time remembering *why* I shouldn't do exactly that as I stare up at Ramanu's gorgeous face. Their horns really accentuate the lines of their face and spotlight their high cheekbones. They're *pretty*.

I wrap my fingers around their wrists to keep from reaching for their horns again. To see if they're bluffing or really intend to...I'm not sure what. Plenty of humans have fucked demons, vampires, and a variety of other paranormal beings who are significantly less humanoid. If it's even close to anatomically possible, some human has tried. That kind of thing might not be as common as it used to be, not with it being all but impossible to cross between the realms, but people got stranded on either side of the barriers when they went up.

It doesn't matter. Having sex with this demon is a mistake. I have places to be, a witch to murder, and my family's magic to safeguard. "Get your hands off me."

KATEE ROBERT

"This time."

I don't like the thrill of heat that goes through me in response to the dark promise of their words. *No, Lenora. Bad witch*. I hop off the table when they step back, and I brush my hands over my dress. I chose it carefully, just like I chose all my clothing for the Shadow Market carefully. One must make an impression, after all.

This dress would do Elvira proud. It's black, and the front is a deep V that barely contains my breasts. There's a slit up each side that flashes my over-the-knee boots and a whole lot of thigh when I walk—and makes it easier to walk, fight, or... well, fuck.

I glance at Ramanu, only to find them looking at me again. *Looking* isn't the right word. They might not have eyes in the traditional sense of the word, but they can see me. I'm certain of it. Right now, their face is tilted as if staring at my chest. I have the most foolhardy desire to run my fingers down the fabric of my dress and tug it aside. Just to see what they'd do. "Eyes are up here, demon."

"You cut a fine figure, little witch."

I refuse to blush with pleasure at the compliment. *Refuse.*

Instead, I turn my attention to how we're going to get into the Shadow Market. Every year, some entrances stay the same and some shift. There aren't any stationary ones close to me, so I pull out my compact mirror and draw my finger over it in a finding spell. This small magic doesn't require blood, but I used up enough summoning Ramanu that it leaves me a little dizzy.

The image shifts, morphing into a map from a bird's-eye view. A bright yellow line courses from our current location to one several blocks away. I snort. "It *would* be a haunted house."

Night has long since fallen. I glance at Ramanu. "If anyone asks, you're just really into costumes and cosplay."

They shrug. "If you're sure. I could also..." They shimmer, and a tall person stands in their place with long blond hair, a square jaw that looks like I could break my fist on, and... I blink and realize I know that face. It graced the cover of many of the old romance novels my gran kept stashed in the attic.

I shake my head. "Absolutely not. Please tell me you don't wear *that* form out."

"It creates quite the reaction."

"I'll just bet it does," I mutter.

"My other go-to is actually my favorite." They shimmer again, and I'm looking into the face of a slightly taller version of a blond who was very famous back in the day for running down the beach in slow motion. They grin. "What do you think?"

I think if they leave the house wearing that illusion, they'll cause a riot. I swallow hard. "Your normal form is fine. It's Halloween, after all." I stalk for the stairs. "Keep up."

They drop the illusion and shadow me up the stairs. I catch them peering about as I duck into the closet and grab a pointed hat. Ramanu laughs when I set it on my head. "And you have the audacity to criticize *my* disguises? Taking yourself a bit seriously, aren't you?"

"It's my costume." I scoop my bag off the floor and toss it over my shoulder. It's heavy as fuck, but I don't have portal magic. There's plenty to buy at the Shadow Market if I forget anything, but like most witches I know, I prefer to use my own tools whenever possible. "Let's go."

I only moved into this house a few months ago, so I'm strangely pleased to see trick-or-treaters crowding the sidewalks. I'm an only child, and I have no desire to birth children of my own, but one of my exes has two kids I adore. We broke up because she wanted me to put away the darker magics and didn't understand they're built into my framework, but Olivia and I are still on a mostly good terms even though she's dating someone who's just as sweet as she is. I get to see the kids sometimes. I wonder if they're out tonight before they attend the market. Surely they're not too old to play pretend? I honestly can't remember their ages. The realization leaves me a bit hollow.

I wasn't sure I even wanted to date someone with kids, and now I find myself missing them?

How strange.

"Thinking dark thoughts."

I jerk my gaze to Ramanu and realize I stopped on the walkway between my house and the street. Some of the children stop to stare at the demon, but the adults with their group hurry them along, shooting us looks ranging from admiring to disapproving.

No, not us. *Me.*

I look down at my far-too-sexy-for-trick-or-treating dress and laugh a little. "Just the ghosts of the past. It's nothing." Olivia is happy now with her cute little midwife who bakes bread on the weekends. It's a better match than we ever were. I'm happy for them. Truly.

I only thought about poisoning her new girlfriend once or half a dozen times. It's not like I *did* it.

"Lenora."

I silently curse myself and start forward in my spike-heeled boots. "Keep up, demon."

The "haunted" house is a normal house so covered in Halloween decorations, it's nearly impossible to see its proper shape. Someone spent a fortune in fake spiderwebs and several smoke machines. It's a little tacky but in a fun way. Gods, I love this holiday.

There's a line out the front and curving around the block. It's tempting to ignore it and walk straight to the entrance, but there's no reason to bring more attention to us than we're already getting. Ramanu studies the line and then follows me to the back of it. "Lots of humans. Lots of nonhumans, too."

"It's a convenient entrance for the people who live in this area."

They turn their attention to the house itself. "I can't see anything indicating this is different than the other buildings in the area."

I blink. "Can you sense magic?"

"It's not as simple as that," they say absently. "Magic, emotions, auras. However you want to describe it. Both people and places have them. My mother is bargainer demon, but my parent is gargoyle. I get this little quirk from them. Along with these." They drift a finger over their second set of horns.

My skin heats. If they're saying what I think they're saying... "*Exactly* what can you see? Or sense? Or whatever?"

They focus back on me, a slow smile pulling at the edges of their lips. "I could see your lust earlier, little witch. So thick, I could taste it on my tongue."

My skin heats, but I refuse to look away. "Emotions aren't intention."

"No," they agree easily. "But they're the first seed of action."

I'd like to say they're dead wrong and I wouldn't be so foolish as to jump into bed with a bargainer demon. Unfortunately, I know myself well enough to acknowledge I am exactly that foolish when it comes to love. Or at least when it comes to lust.

Dangerous, sweet, cuttingly ambitious. No one would gather my exes into a room and immediately draw a line of similarities between them. The only thing they have in common is being utterly unsuitable for *me*. Even so, Ramanu would win the prize for most unsuitable. They don't even live in this realm.

And they want seven years of my life.

"Not this time." I try to say it firmly, but it comes out almost like a question.

Their grin goes downright wolfish, and they ease a little closer. "Come now, Lenora. Sign my contract and come away with me. Sex and games and maybe even some murder thrown in to spice things up. It would be fun."

Of that, I have no doubt. The chemistry sizzles between us like a live wire and we've barely touched. I give myself a shake and glance at the line. It's moved quite a bit while I was distracted with Ramanu. "Let's go."

Neither of us speaks as the line inches its way to the entrance of the house. It's a relatively quick process. The woman who's dressed as an angel and is dividing the groups has a glint in her eye that isn't quite human, and when she surveys Ramanu, I'm sure of it. "Nice *costume*."

"Thanks." They smile sweetly. "I like yours, too." Is that flirtation in their tone?

I'm bristling, and I have no right to bristle. Nothing about this evening is going right. "We want the special pass."

She finally focuses on me. "Of course." She rips a ticket from the roll in her hand and waves it through the air. A shimmer sizzles over it, there and gone again in an instant. She hands it over. "Follow your number."

I glance at it and roll my eyes. "Sixty-nine. Really?"

She shrugs. "You get what you get. Go ahead."

Ramanu falls in behind me as I approach the door. There are more fake cobwebs strung about inside, thick enough that I hope someone has cleaning magic, or they'll be finding bits of it for years to come. Arrows made of glow-in-the-dark tape point us down the narrow hall lined with doors. I take one step and stop short. "Hey, Ramanu."

"Yes?" They're so close, I can almost feel the heat from their body against my back.

I look over my shoulder. "You know how a haunted house works, right? They jump out, we scream, they go away. No murdering the actors."

"Spoilsport."

I narrow my eyes. "I'm serious. And don't wander. I imagine there are a lot of portals in this place, and even *you* won't want to end up where some of them lead."

They hesitate then finally nod. "I'll attempt to keep the murder to a minimum and will follow along like a dutiful pup."

That's not exactly the reassurance I was looking for, but I suppose it'll have to do. "Good puppy." As soon as the words leave my lips, I regret them. Dear gods, am I *flirting* with this demon? I snap back to face the front. I'm not in the habit of feeling shame, but I just got done telling myself to leave this demon alone, yet my first instinct is still to shift closer and look up at their fascinating face and tip my head back and...

Ugh. *No.*

I charge forward, following the taped arrows. The first room is done up like a doctor's exam room. A human jumps out from behind the table, a saw in one hand and fake blood covering their surgical scrubs. Behind me, I feel Ramanu tense. "Back the fuck off," I snarl.

The human stops short. "Jesus, lady, if you're not going to play, why are you here?"

Because this is the closest portal into the Shadow Market. I ignore them and keep moving through the door and down another hall. It takes three more rooms and three more aborted attempts to startle me before we reach the stairs to the second floor.

Ramanu chuckles. "The poor humans are right. They put so much work into this. The least you could do is give a cute little scream."

"I don't give cute little screams." I check my pace to avoid going up the stairs two at a time. Gods forbid the demon think I'm running from them. "These kinds of places hold nothing for me."

"I'm beginning to see that."

No telling what that tone means, so I ignore it. The stairs lead to a hallway with a dozen doors. "Now we're getting somewhere." In the distance, screams sound. I pause. Those don't sound like fun screams. They sound like someone's being murdered...or maybe stumbled onto a real body. I shrug. Not my problem.

Though usually the fun with humans doesn't start until they're through the various portals to their final destinations.

Near the end of the hall, a number shimmers on a door, drawing my attention. Sixty-nine. I roll my eyes. "This way."

We stop in front of it, and Ramanu lifts their head, inhaling deeply. "I smell blood."

"Seems like someone got a bit overeager. They'll figure it out." I reach for the door. "Or maybe another hellcat will rampage through this place like happened a few decades ago. That was quite the mess, to hear my fathers tell it."

"You don't care about the poor, defenseless humans."

I stop short and glare. Their tone isn't exactly judgmental, but it's not neutral, either. "I'm sorry, but you don't get to take that high and mighty tone with me. Your whole thing is taking advantage of humans by making deals with them."

"You say we're taking advantage. I say we offer them an escape from a desperate situation."

"To the tune of seven years."

Ramanu snorts. "If anything, it's giving away something they wouldn't have had to begin with. Seven extra years rather than seven years lost. Beyond that, *I'm* not a human. You are. You not caring about your people is more eyebrow raising than anything I do."

I twist the handle on the door. "That's the thing, Ramanu. If you can sense magic the way you claim, then you'd know most witches aren't all human. We couldn't wield magic if we were." I push the door open and step out of the haunted house into the Shadow Market.

CHAPTER 4

RAMANU

My little witch isn't very happy with me, but the onslaught of energy that slaps me in the face the moment we walk through the door nearly makes me forget it. I've traveled the length of this realm and several others. Every space feels a bit different, the flavors of magic influenced by the people who reside there.

This place feels like all of them combined.

It sets me back on my heels as my brain and inherent magic try to sort and process all the information. I quickly realize it's impossible. Every time I almost have a handle on it, the energy shifts as some new person or element is introduced.

Meanwhile, Lenora hasn't paused to wait for me. She's moving forward, her energy snapping around her in an almost feral way.

I take half a second to intentionally mute the greater swirls of color and information. If something dangerous or noteworthy happens, I'll sense it, but this allows me to focus only on what's directly around me.

We've stepped out into an open-air market. This section seems designated for food, because delicious smells weave through the air from the nearby stalls. The witch, of course, marches right past them. I ignore the way my mouth waters and follow her.

People get out of our way. It takes ten steps before Lenora realizes it and spins to face me. Irritation is a burnt orange. "Stop glowering at everyone. You're making a scene."

"They're not scared of *me*, little witch."

She pauses, her face appearing in a starburst of light-orange shock and deep forest-green pride. "Yes, well, keep up." She huffs and surges forward again.

As predicted, people get out of her way. I detect a myriad of paranormals in the area, from vampires to a few I have a hard time putting name to. All in Lenora's path find somewhere else to be, their energies shifting away from us.

Something akin to pride settles in my chest. *My witch is quite the fearsome little thing, isn't she?* Not that she's particularly little, but compared to me, most people in this place are. They breed them small in the human realm. I'm not particularly tall among *my* people.

I follow her through the market as the scents change from food to leather and magic. Which is where Lenora stops short and her deep forest green disappears, leaving only the light orange. "Jack. You're early."

"I'm not early. You're late. As always." The person in front of her is a sunny yellow. I get the impression of short curly hair, an ample body, and a bright grin. Human but flavored similar to Lenora. *Witch.*

Lenora sighs, the sound almost imperceptible in the greater noise of the market. "Ramanu, this is Jack. They're a friend."

"Friend." Jack laughs. "Darling, you're really hedging your bets, aren't you?" They throw an arm around Lenora's shoulders, and I have the nearly overwhelming impulse to rip it off their body and beat them to death with it.

Lenora doesn't shrug out of their grip, her shock changing to a deep yellow amusement. "Jack, this is Ramanu. They're, ah, also a friend."

"A *horny* friend."

"For fuck's sake, Jack."

Jack extends their hand, and I reluctantly take it, just as reluctantly beating back to urge to squeeze too tightly. This is ridiculous. I want the little witch, but she's not mine. Not yet, anyways. Surely I'm not threatened by some adorable human who's overly familiar with her?

Liar.

"What Lenora isn't saying is that we used to bang seven ways to Sunday and now we're friends, and if you pull some shady demon shit with her, I'll curse the fuck out of you. I'm the best curse worker in this hemisphere, and so trust me, you don't want that."

I'm not certain what it says about me that I find their threats charming. I grin. "If I pull some *nasty demon shit* with Lenora, she's more than capable of handling me herself."

Jack considers me for a long moment and laughs. "I like this demon." They turn back to Lenora. "You're sure you want to try this?"

Lenora sighs. "I don't have a choice." Gray worry starts to eat the edges of her amusement. "If you've changed your mind—"

"I haven't. Fuck that smug bastard. I know he's gorgeous and all, but honestly, Len. So is a saber-tooth tiger, and you wouldn't sleep with one of them."

"Yes, you've already lectured me about it. Several times."

That strange protective urge rises again. "Surely you're not saying it's *Lenora's* fault."

"Of course not. I'm just talking." Jack curses. "Look, I said I'm going to help, and I will. Don't try to talk me out of it."

Lenora gives them a quick hug. "I appreciate you."

"Of course you do. I'm a gift." They hesitate. "But this is something you should probably know."

Lenora goes light orange. "What are you talking about?"

Jack's a red shot through with a sickly yellow green. I get the impression of round cheeks and hard eyes. "*Everyone* knows. He's waltzing around here wearing your family's amulet and bragging about how you fell so in love with him that you handed it over."

"That is *not* what happened."

"Oh, I know." Jack sighs. "You wouldn't part with that thing for love or money, and you're too cold to let a good fucking cloud your mind enough to pass it over. But knowing the truth doesn't stop him from spreading the lie."

"I'm going to kill that motherfucker." Her orange shifts to a red so deep, it's nearly black. "Excuse me, Jack. I've got somewhere to be."

"Hey, Len." Jack waits for her to pause to continue. "Be careful. There's some weird stuff going on this time around. The opening ceremony was more complicated than normal, and—"

"That has nothing to do with me." Lenora turns and stalks through the crowd, a sharp knife ready to strike.

"Ramanu."

I want to follow my witch, but I make myself pause and turn to Jack. "Yes?"

"I don't know what you're doing with Lenora or what you're up to, but I get the feeling you don't actually mean her harm."

I focus in on them, narrowing my attention until...ah, there it is. "Telepath."

"Something like that." I get the impression of a shark-sharp smile. "Which is why I know you've got a thing for my ex. Watch her back, demon. I wasn't kidding about the curse work."

I nod and allow the crowd to bear me away from them, following Lenora. She's the only one deep red in the mix of colors and sensations around me. More than that, I have the taste of her now.

I'd like the taste of her literally.

She veers around a stall, and I follow her through a series of narrow streets that aren't quite streets. The marketplace gives way to more permanent buildings. A few of them are restaurants and pubs, but Lenora bypasses them all, only slowing when we reach a quieter street that feels familiar. Temporary lodgings have the same sensation regardless of which time or territory or realm you're in.

Lenora pauses. She's still angry, but there's a spiderweb of light gray through the deep color that I don't like. I don't want my witch scared. Before I can speak, she holds up a hand. "Is it safe to say I'm not losing you this weekend?"

"Are you trying to lose me?" I'm genuinely curious. She's powerful enough to banish me if she really wanted to, and not just because she summoned me in the first place.

"No." That thread of fear in her gets stronger even as she makes an obvious attempt to shake it off. "I have no intention of making a deal with you, Ramanu. But...I'm not someone who fails. I can't afford to do so with Kristoff. Not again. So I guess you're the ace up my sleeve, poison though it may be."

"Lenora." I slowly close the distance between us. Each step, the gray of fear retreats a little more until I stop nearly touching her. "Seven years of pleasure."

Shock. Wide eyes and lips parted. "Excuse me?"

"Seven years of pleasure." I don't touch her. I told her I wouldn't, but I didn't expect it to be this challenging to control the urge to grab her hips and bring her flush to my body. "This doesn't have to be a deal where anyone loses. I want you. I think you want me, too."

The bright pink of lust starts to eat away at the edges of

her anger. "You can't be serious. Bargainer demons are making *sex pacts*?"

"No, of course not." If one tried, Azazel would skin them alive. "The terms of the deal are that you would come to my realm for the duration of seven years and be under my protection. No one would force you to do anything, and no harm would come to you."

"Uh-huh." Amusement creeps in, but lust still holds dominant. "Isn't that a bit of a conflict of interest? If the deal is to protect me, then who's going to protect me from *you*?"

A fair question. It's a nonissue, but I don't expect her to believe that. "The contract is sacred. Its magic will ensure you're not harmed in any way."

"Sure it will." Lenora laughs. It's a wicked sound, filled with barbs and sharp edges. I like it. A lot. "And I'm supposed to believe a few hours in my presence is enough to make you want to give me *seven years of pleasure*. Please. I realize it doesn't look that way with this situation with Kristoff, but I'm not a fool."

"I never said you were a fool."

"Not in so many words, but you're saying it nonetheless."

"Look over the contract, little witch. What harm can it bring?"

She flicks her hair over her shoulder, sending up a thread of something earthy that must be her shampoo. "That's the question, isn't it?" She shakes her head. "Regardless, I have a room and you don't. It doesn't matter if you have money tucked away because these rooms book up years in advance. So are you going to behave and stay in my room, or shall I leave you to haunt the market while I take a nap?"

As if there's even the slightest question. "I'll behave." I grin. "Until you ask me not to."

"Yeah, that's what I thought." She snorts. "Come up. I'll read your contract."

As I follow her through the door and into the charmingly magicked front room of the inn, I can't help wondering what Lenora's motivation is in this. She says I'm the poisoned ace up her sleeve, but if that's the case, why not make it a sure thing and bargain with me? She's failed three times to kill Kristoff. She's formidable, but I don't see her succeeding in future attempts, either.

Then there's her fear.

What is this amulet to her? That's the one question I haven't been able to answer in the process of circling my witch. I thought it as simple as a family heirloom, but if that were the case, Kristoff wouldn't be parading it around. Others wouldn't recognize it on sight.

Lenora chats briefly with the old witch at the front desk and then lifts her voice. "Come, demon." As I approach, she laughs. "As you can see, they're perfectly well-behaved."

The witch looks me over, and I can see her clearly through the swirl of pink and deep yellow. "I certainly hope not. It seems a waste of a good bargainer demon to be *well-behaved*."

"Um."

The witch waves in the direction of the stairs. "We have brownies on staff, so don't think about stealing. They take tips in sweets."

"We'll keep that in mind," Lenora says faintly.

"See that you do."

It doesn't take long to find Lenora's room. *Our* room. The thought pleases me far more than it should. To distract myself and stay on topic, I shut the door and lean against it. "What's so special about this amulet, Lenora?"

She freezes, fear once again taking hold. I *hate* that she's afraid. "It's nothing."

"Don't lie to me. If I'm your secret last-ditch effort, then I need to have all the information. There's something I need to know about the amulet, isn't there?"

"Fine," she snaps. "It's celestial made. Anyone who wears it can't be killed by poison or magic. There's a decent chance they also can't be harmed by violence, but that's never been conclusively proven. It's why Kristoff's managed to dodge my attempts so far."

She's not telling the whole truth. I knew there was a protection spell in the amulet—it seems to be common knowledge. "What else?"

"That's it." Her magic snaps against mine. "No one else would have dared steal it, but I was foolish enough to fall asleep next to Kristoff, and that's exactly what he did."

That same strange jealousy that arose with Jack's presence takes root and dives deep. I clench my fists, wanting nothing more than to rip this bastard's head off for abusing my witch's trust. It doesn't make a damn bit of sense.

I've loved and lost and all that; one doesn't move through the world without touching others and making impressions made in return. I've never been territorial. Except it's not entirely territorial—*that* would make a bit of sense. I'm jealous of how familiar Jack was, yes, but I'm infuriated by how Kristoff has harmed Lenora.

He took away her protection, and he used her trust to do it.

No wonder fear takes hold whenever she thinks about the amulet. It's a powerful protection and given to her by her fathers. Still... My instincts say there's more to the story. "Celestial made."

"Yes. A distant ancestor of mine was beloved by a god. This was the gift. It doesn't affect aging or anything like that, but it's one of the most powerful protection items in existence." Her voice is stiff. "I realize it was foolish to let him so close, but—"

"You don't have to justify yourself to me, little witch." I move past her and pull out the chair next to the desk. "Sit.

Read over the contract." With a flourish and a pull of my magic, it appears on the desk.

Suspicion takes root, but she finally does as I say and sinks into the chair. While she reads over the contract, I consider the fucked-up position I'm now in. If Lenora agrees to a bargain with me, it will be on the condition I retrieve the amulet for her.

That's the problem, though.

If the amulet is celestial and around the neck of this particular witch, there's a good chance I *can't* retrieve it. I won't be able to use magic against him, which means it will be a brute-force scenario. That leaves a lot more to chance than doing things my preferred way—using my magic to prevail. I can't guarantee a win.

Fuck.

CHAPTER 5

LENORA

Color me shocked, but the language in the contract is exactly what Ramanu promised. The payment is seven years of service, yes, but it's clearly spelled out that no harm can come to me and no one can force me to do anything I don't want. There's a horrifying little clause about children resulting from any sex I choose to have while in the demon realm, but I have no interest in procreating, so that's a nonissue.

It doesn't mean I'm going to agree to the bargain.

I shouldn't have summoned Ramanu. It was a mistake to let fear take hold. I have three days to get the amulet back from Kristoff, and with the help of Jack and the others, I should be able to do it without sacrificing seven years.

Then why haven't you banished Ramanu? You know how to do it.

I ignore the snide little voice inside me and read over the contract a second time.

Ramanu drifts around the room, taking up far too much space. It's not even their size, though demons tend to be built larger than humans. It's their energy. I can't see magic the way they can, but I feel like I'm tuned to every move they make. It's not unpleasant, but it's distracting.

I slip my hand into my pocket for the slip of paper Jack left me when they hugged me close. There's no point trying to hide what I'm doing from the demon, so I take it out and unfold it. There, in Jack's messy scrawl, is a short list of times and places.

"What's that?"

I don't jump at Ramanu's voice in my ear. They weren't quiet with their approach. "This is where Kristoff will be during the next two and a half days." The first time is tonight at midnight, which means we have time to kill. The market is an all-hours thing, but the night is when things truly get wild.

I'd joked about a nap, but it's probably a good idea. I didn't sleep much last night—too amped with plans and contingency plans and more contingency plans for my contingency plans. Nowhere in all that strategizing was I where I am now.

Sharing a room with a bargainer demon who wants to give me *pleasure* for the next seven years.

Yeah, right. Surely Ramanu doesn't think I was born yesterday? They can offer pleasure all they want, but it's not in the contract, which means it's not guaranteed.

"Can the amulet be stolen?"

I blink and try to pull my mind back to the present. "Yes. It's how Kristoff took it from me in the first place. I *never* would have given it to him or anyone else." It's been passed from parent to child in the Byrne family for generations. The connection to the bloodlines ensures the magic stays strong. Since I have no desire to procreate, I'll have to find a distant cousin to pass it on to when I'm ready. There are plenty of them scattered across the globe.

But I won't be able to pass on the amulet if I don't *have* the amulet. I need it back. The sooner, the better. My fathers are hardly as plugged into the paranormal gossip circuit as they used to be, but even they'll hear about this if Kristoff still has the amulet by the end of Samhain. Worse, at some point we'll start feeling the effects of its absence. I don't know if our magic will disappear completely, not with our varied lineage littered with paranormals, but I honestly can't guarantee anything. I need to reclaim the amulet before we have a chance to find out.

The pressure and stress bear down on me, tighter and heavier, a blanket of suffocating fear that I can barely breathe past. This has to work. I *have* to get it back. I can't be the one who ruined generations' worth of safety because of a good fuck.

I'm a screwup.

I know that.

I'm not the kind of daughter my fathers had hoped for, and while they've never chastised me or wielded their disappointment as a weapon, I *know* it's there beneath the surface.

This mistake might be the one that breaks the dam that's been building since Da found me with that dead bird when I was twelve. I hadn't killed it, but I'd found my great-grandmother's grimoire at that stage, and there's plenty of magic in it that requires blood. I wanted to test a glamour spell.

I'll never forget the look on his face, the way he blanched and then gently removed the knife from my hand and urged me to my feet. I didn't try the spell that afternoon. Instead, we buried the bird.

If I were a good daughter, one to be proud of, that would have been enough to steer me onto a different path. Unfortunately, I'm a bit too much like my great-grandmother.

"Lenora?" The concern in Ramanu's voice nearly undoes me.

I can't take their pity. But, with my emotions coating me

like a blanket of spikes, there is something I will take from them. If they're willing.

I push slowly to my feet. I already know I'm not going to be able to sleep. Not right now, not with this tangled mess making ugly work in my brain. The smart thing would be to dig through my bag for a sleeping tea and brew myself a cup. To resign myself to the nightmares that will inevitably follow. A small price to pay, I suppose.

I'm not feeling very smart right now.

"Ramanu."

They go still, and I shiver as all their attention narrows on me. "Yes?"

It takes more effort than I'll ever admit not to fidget. I lift my chin. This is a mistake, but I'm a train hurtling out of control toward a ruined bridge. It's too late to stop. "You really think seven years of pleasure is enough to turn my head?"

They seem to stop breathing. "You seem to have a suggestion. Let's hear it."

My long-ignored common sense tries to speak up, but I ignore it. Already, my sadness is sharpening to lust. It's such a relief, I could weep. Ever since I woke up in Kristoff's empty bed without the familiar weight of my amulet, fear and loathing have dogged my every step. I can't escape the feelings, not until I recover what was taken from me.

But...I could allow myself a reprieve, couldn't I? A small break before I go back to feeling like the failure I am. "You can't really expect to sell that sort of promise without a trial run, can you?"

"A trial run." Ramanu grins, quick and wicked. "Shall we bargain, little witch?"

"Not for seven years."

"No." They shake their head. "Not for seven years. Not

for this. You want a trial run, which is well within your right to request."

I really should laugh it off and let this go. I don't. Instead, I nod. "Yes. Really, it's a selling point as far as you're concerned. Unless you were bullshitting me..."

"I wasn't." They take another step toward me. "Bargain with me, Lenora." The way they say it almost sounds like an invitation to foreplay.

I shiver. "I'm spelled with birth control, if that's necessary."

Ramanu circles me slowly. Never closing the distance. More like they're trying to get my measure. "I have no desire to trap you there. Children are for others. I want none of my own."

I twist to face them. "I like kids. I even trained with a midwife for a while." My fathers' insistence. They wanted to ensure I had a good balanced foundation before I chose what kind of magic I wanted to specialize in. A last-ditch effort to guide me to life and light instead of the fixation I have with darker magics. "I just don't want them myself."

Ramanu reaches out and catches a lock of my hair before running it through their clawed fingers. "A month."

It shocks me how much I want to say yes. I've known this demon a few hours and I'm willing to give them a month? I shake my head, dislodging their touch. "You get an hour."

Far from being dissuaded, Ramanu seems to relish the bartering. "Two weeks."

I find myself smiling. "This afternoon, ending when I need to go track down Kristoff."

"Please. An afternoon is hardly enough, and we both know it. You can feel this connection, too."

They're right. I've never felt anything quite like this before. If so much of my energy weren't wrapped up in getting the amulet back, I'd probably be terrified. My laugh is a little too edged. "I feel a lot of things. That doesn't mean I'm going to give you two weeks."

"Fair enough." They hold up three fingers. "Three days. The duration of Samhain. At the end of the Shadow Market, you'll make your decision about the greater bargain."

"I already made my decision."

They shrug, but the movement is as practiced as my laugh. Tension builds between us. We both know we'll reach an agreement, which means we both know what comes next. They grin. "Then it won't change in the next three days."

They have a point, but that doesn't mean I have to like it. "Fine. Three days." I frown. "I don't want marks of any kind on my body."

They stop behind me and catch my hips, their claws pressing lightly against me. "Not even little bruises?" They lean down and murmur in my ear, "Not even a tiny memory of where I held you down and fucked you?"

Damn them, but it's like they're speaking directly to the lust coursing through me with increasing strength. I shiver. "Little bruises are fine. No claw marks. No blood. And nothing that can't be covered by clothing." The last thing I want to do is confront Kristoff with hickeys or something from Ramanu.

Though the thought isn't *entirely* unappealing.

"Deal," Ramanu says. Their lips brush the shell of my ear. "You may leave marks on me. In fact, I would deeply enjoy wearing your claw marks." They catch my wrist before lifting and turning it to examine my long nails.

"They're magically reinforced and sharpened." I don't get into as many catfights as I used to when I was in my early twenties and drinking entirely too much, but old habits die hard.

"Perfect." Their breath shudders out. "I like a bit of pain, but don't maim me."

"I have no interest in maiming you." I've never done anything like this before. Oh, there have been plenty of conversations about limits and desires, but this feels different. Almost as if with every question and counteroffer, Ramanu is building a spell around just us two. It's not magic, though. I can sense nothing in the air but our mutual lust.

"Lenora." Their hand flexes on my hip. "May I come inside you?"

I turn to face them and carefully press my hands to their chest. We haven't even kissed yet, haven't taken off a single article of clothing, and I'm already shaking with need. Who knew negotiations could be this sexy? "It's on the table." I smile slowly. "But you'll have to work for it."

It's only because I'm touching them that I feel their shiver. I love that Ramanu is so deeply affected by this. It makes me want to see what else deeply affects them. "Horns?" I ask.

"They're not more sensitive than the rest of me, but I feel it when you touch them." I reach up, and they lean down so I can drag my finger along one. Ramanu gives another of those delicious shivers and answers my unspoken question. "Yes, I like it."

I drop my hand. "Is there any terminology you'd prefer I use for your body? Or not use?" The last thing I want is to do is say something wrong and jar Ramanu out of a good time. I want us both to enjoy this from beginning to end.

Their smile is so sweet, it lights up their face. "I appreciate the ask, but I'm not precious about language. Use what you'd like."

"Okay." I take a step back. Their hand tightens on my hip and then releases me as I take another. "I think that's enough for negotiations, don't you?" This dress was designed to be shed easily; it only takes two flicks before it's sliding down my body to pool around my ankles.

I start to reach for my boots, but Ramanu shakes their head sharply. "Keep them on."

"If you'd like." I sit on the bed and scoot backward to the middle of it. After the briefest hesitation, I spread my thighs. "I know you can sense things, but—"

"Your lust is so strong, it's a very clear picture." They unbutton their shirt with quick, efficient movements, the fabric parting to reveal a bitable crimson chest with red nipples so dark, they're almost black. Their pants and boots quickly follow. Then they pause, allowing me to look my fill.

Gods, Ramanu really is pretty.

There's muscle definition in their shoulders, arms, athletic thighs, and shapely calves. This demon doesn't skip leg day. Clawed feet give me pause, only because I hadn't registered that their boots were shaped differently than human boots. I skate my gaze up to their hips, where their cock is so hard, it looks painful. It's a nice cock. Thick and long with a wicked curve that makes me shiver. "Get over here, Ramanu."

They don't move. "Negotiations remain open throughout the process."

"Sure." I nod and reach between my spread thighs to stroke my clit. They've barely touched me and I'm already halfway there. "If I do something you don't like, tell me."

They laugh. "Of course, little witch. The same goes for you." They move to the edge of the bed and plant their hands on either side of my hips. "Use your words. Don't blast me across the room."

"Not even a little blast?" My voice has gone breathy and low. I don't stop stroking myself, and the way they inhale deeply as if tasting my desire on the air between us nearly has me coming on the spot.

"You're the one paying for damages to the hotel room." Their voice has lowered, too. It's just us in the room, and we're both naked, but suddenly this feels a thousand times more intimate. "As I said, I don't mind pain in bedroom games."

"Noted," I manage.

They dip, their horns brushing over my breasts and down my stomach as they urge my thighs wider and settle between them. "Spread your pussy for me, little witch."

I make a V with my fingers and obey without thinking, spreading my folds for them. They inhale deeply again. "You may hang on if you like." They lower their head and drag their tongue over me. I lift my hand, and they suck my fingers into their mouth. Ramanu makes a deep sound in their throat and releases my fingers to duck down and seal their mouth over my pussy.

"Oh gods."

I don't get a chance to *hang on*. Ramanu lifts their head and grabs my thighs, guiding me to drape my legs over their horns. This time, when they dip back down, they force my legs up and back as they do. Baring me completely. "Pretty little thing," they murmur against my heated flesh.

Then their tongue is there, dragging up my center to roll against my clit. After all the pressure and fear and stress from the past couple weeks, the sheer pleasure almost hurts. It's too good and not enough, all at the same time. "More!"

Ramanu shifts higher, and then their fingers are at my entrance. I tense, thinking of the claws, but when they press into me, there's no sharpness or pain. Just a fullness that has me arching my back and whimpering.

There's no time to wonder how I got here, about the series of decisions that resulted in me naked but for my boots, a demon fucking me with their fingers as they work my clit with their tongue.

As pleasure winds through me tighter and tighter, I edge into that space where Ramanu could ask me anything and I'd say yes as long as they didn't stop until I cum.

They don't ask for anything. They just keep at me until I orgasm with their name on my lips. They ease their fingers out of me and give my pussy one last thorough kiss. I think they intend to move up my body, but it's like that second taste holds them captive. They moan and settle back between my thighs.

"Ramanu," I gasp.

They ignore me, other than to work their thick tongue into me. I whimper, but we only have so much time before I need to get ready to leave the room. I love this, but I want more, and I'm getting the feeling that, if left to their own devices, they'd spent all the allotted time eating me out.

Maybe another time.

I ignore the voice that tries to point out we only have three days. Not even three full days since the Shadow Market started at midnight last night and we showed up this afternoon.

Another wave of pleasure builds inside me. It's so tempting to just submit. To let them get me there as many times as they'd like. I should...

I slap my hand against the sharp point of one of their horns. The pain makes me suck in a breath, and Ramanu freezes. They lift their head. "Lenora—"

I bite out the magic command and feel the answering tug in my palm. The response is immediate. Black ribbons appear and wrap around Ramanu's arms and legs. I flex my fist, wincing at the pain, and the ribbons snap tight, flipping Ramanu onto their back. If I weren't tangled up in their horns, the quick change in position would have sent me flying, but I end up kneeling over their face.

They flex their fists, pulling against the ribbons. "Neat trick."

"It serves its purpose." I carefully move back so I can straddle their stomach and then stand and move to the edge of the bed. "You paint quite the pretty picture." It's the truth.

They're spread-eagle on the bed, their body completely at my mercy. Their cock bobs a bit as I kneel between their thighs. "Maybe I should keep you like this for the next three days."

They flex again, giving another tug on the constraints. "You hold me because I consent to being held."

I don't expect the simple statement to shake me to my core. I've had a wide range of sexual partners for a variety of reasons. Love, lust, even hate occasionally. Most of the time, even when love was involved, I was achingly aware of any power imbalance. I have to be careful with those less powerful than me. For those who are more powerful? It's always a push and pull and intricate dance to protect myself while I'm at my most vulnerable.

If I tried this on one of *them*, they would have slashed through the ribbons or torn them out at the seams and then immediately done something to counter and flip the power balance again. To give proof that they weren't helpless, even for sex games.

Ramanu isn't exactly submitting, but they're allowing me to take the lead for the time being. It's...refreshing.

I lightly drag my fingernails over their thighs. They let their head fall back to the bed, and I have a moment to sigh over the holes their horns punch in the comforter. That will be expensive, but it's worth it to see the long line of their throat exposed. To have them willingly putting themself at my mercy.

To have them...trusting me.

At least in this.

CHAPTER 6

RAMANU

"Pain for the sake of pain? Or pain to spice pleasure?"

It takes several beats for Lenora's low voice to penetrate the fog of lust clouding my thoughts. I had a moment where I almost instinctively shredded the ribbons she summoned. I'm very glad I didn't. My little witch is practically preening as she alternates between massaging my thighs and lightly stroking them with her sharp nails.

And they are sharp. Magically reinforced and able to shred flesh if she's so inclined. It's a token of how far gone I am that I'm not worried about how close those nails are to my nether bits.

I suck in a breath. "The latter."

"Good to know," she murmurs. Lenora leans down and takes my length into her mouth. My whole body goes tight as she sucks me down, down, down. It shouldn't be possible for her to take all of me like this, but her lips meet my base, and she hums happily.

Then the little witch rakes her nails down my thighs, scoring me deeply.

I cry out.

Pleasure and pain twine together as she sucks me hard. I dig my heels into the mattress, trying to hold out, to fight against the growing pressure and tightness. Fuck. If she doesn't stop, I'm going to cum, and then...

I'm not ready for this to stop.

A jerk of my arms and the ribbons holding them snap. I dig one hand into her hair and haul her off me. "Come here."

"Bossy." But she doesn't fight me as I lift her to straddle my hips. I wrap a fist around myself, and then I'm at her entrance. Though the little witch didn't need to fight to take me in her mouth, she's fighting now. She whimpers and rolls her hips, sinking inch after slow inch down. I try to arch up, but the ribbons around my legs hold me immobile.

I could snap them like I snapped the others, but I like this. I like how her magic swirls around us, electric pink and sunny yellow. I like feeling held down by her. She runs her hands down my chest and back up again. Her nails prick me, but only that. "You feel good."

"Ride me, little witch. I want to feel you cum again."

Lenora arches back and presses her hands to my thighs, squeezing the cuts as she picks up her pace. The pain surges again, and I surge with it. I grab her hips and slam her down onto me. She responds by digging her fingers in harder, though distantly I note she's not using her nails this time.

Very well. Two can play that game.

"You don't feel like working, little witch?" I laugh hoarsely and lift her again. "Very well. You can play my little fuck toy, and I'll use you until I'm satisfied."

She gasps. "Do it."

I release her hips long enough to wedge my hands between us and wrap my fingers around her ass. The new position forces her legs out and takes away what little stability she had. I lift her until she's nearly free of me. "Put your feet on my shoulders. Hold my horns."

As soon as she obeys, I start to work her back down my length. I'm holding her entire weight, and she makes a delicious little whimpering sound as I bottom out inside her. I don't give her a chance to adjust to it, though. Instead, I lift her again, using her to fuck me. Slowly. It takes everything I have, but I'm determined to go slow, to enjoy every moment of this.

The sharp heels of her boots dig into my shoulders, pinpricks of pain that urge me to go faster. Harder. I fight to ignore the impulse. "Cum for me, little witch. Let me feel it."

"Make me."

I laugh hoarsely. Trust her to turn this into a battle as well. I like that about Lenora. She's all sharp edges and flaring power. I've always liked my partners to have claws, usually literally.

With the little witch, something's different, though. There's a soft center there. She doesn't show it often, but her emotions tell the truth of her. It's a contrast that draws me despite myself. *She* draws me.

I keep using her to fuck me. It takes three strokes to find the exact angle that makes her head fall back and her long hair brush my torn thighs. She's such a saturated pink right now, I can see every line of her clearly. The roundness of her breasts, the soft curve of her stomach, the glistening wet of her pussy.

Her hands tighten around my horns. "Ramanu," she gasps. "Don't stop! I'm going to—" She cries out loud enough that I'm half-surprised she doesn't shake the paintings from the walls.

It's too much. I slam her down onto me, my body getting the best of my control. I roar my way through my own orgasm, pumping into her until her pussy overflows and my seed coats my bloody thighs.

I wrap my arms around the little witch and arrange her against my chest. She slumps down, her breath a harsh match for mine. The lust swimming about her dims a little, but it's hardly sated.

Lenora blows out a breath and gives a shaky laugh. "Not too shabby, demon."

"You either, little witch." She shifts a little, but I don't drop my arms, and she finally settles back against me. This is... nice. My thighs are already healing, the cuts from her nails sealing shut and the pain fading to nothing. The pleasure takes longer to dim, and even then, it morphs to a deep contentedness that only seems to come after good sex.

I like that she lets me hold her. It's a small intimacy I don't bother engaging in with most of my partners. Intimacy leads to expectations, and I'm too damned ambitious to let a relationship sidetrack me. It took me years to work my way up the ranks high enough to catch Azazel's attention and then years yet to prove myself a reliable resource.

Because of that, *I'm* the one he sends to keep track of the human gifts he manipulated the other territory leaders into taking. A calculated risk, that. There's a reason bargainers don't let the humans we make deals with wander the demon realm these days. Their safety is of the utmost importance.

By allowing them out of our sight and out of our territory, he can't guarantee their safety no matter what promises he made to them. The contract will notify him if something goes awry, but in the seconds it would take him to get to their side, it might already be too late.

I am the, ah, stopgap to deal with that while we wait to see what the other territory leaders will do. My check-ins were a reminder of the consequences for mistreating their gifts. Not all of them have settled perfectly into their new lives, but enough have that Azazel approved this bargain for me.

"Ramanu."

"Mmmm?" I stroke a careful hand through Lenora's long hair.

She lifts her head. "You said seven years would only be a few hours—a month at most."

Surely one round of sex isn't enough to convince her to make the bargain? I force myself not to hold my breath. "Yes."

"Doesn't that mean you're missing out on like...decades over there by staying here for three days? You'll go back, and everyone you know will be dead and gone."

Ah. That. I hesitate, but there's really no harm in her knowing the truth. It's not exactly something we bargainers broadcast, but it's not a secret, either. "The realms don't actually touch. There's a bit of space between them where beings who can realm hop can exert some control over the flow of time. It's not a perfect equation, and it's easier to finesse coming here than it is going back, but I'll only have missed a few weeks." It should be fine. Azazel has others capable of handling anything that comes up.

That doesn't mean *he's* going to be happy with the change of plans, but there's a better-than-decent chance he'll be too preoccupied with Eve...

But then, I've never been a particularly lucky person. It's very likely I'll be punished when I return, regardless of whether I secure this bargain or not.

"I see," Lenora says slowly. She shifts and eases off me. "We should get moving."

"Lenora." I don't know why I say her name like that, dark and full of promise. I've decided I want her for keeping, but there's no reason to signal that ahead of time. She's not the type to run, but I wouldn't put it past her to try and slit my throat. The thought makes me smile. She's so fierce and yet so brittle. It makes me want to wrap her up and keep her safe. "He won't win."

"I know." She walks to the bathroom and shuts the door. I'm only mortal. I like that she stumbles a bit when she does.

As soon as the door shuts, the ribbons binding my legs

turn to smoke and disappear. I climb off the bed and am in the process of considering how to best clean up the mess we made when a light magic blurs through the air. It takes half a heartbeat to register the flavor. Brownie. It sweeps along the bed, eliminating all evidence of fucking and leaving a light citrus scent in the air. Within a minute, the room feels just like it did when we first walked in.

"Neat trick." One less thing to worry about, but I dislike how easy it was to remove traces of us. My thighs are completely healed now, not so much as a scar to show for Lenora's nails. It's a reminder I should take to heart. There's no guarantee the little witch will agree to my bargain, and even if she does, seven years isn't all that long of a time. Regardless of which way one looks at the situation, it's temporary.

The thought shouldn't feel like sharp grains of sand beneath my skin. It's how things work. Even as much as I like what I know of Lenora, that doesn't change the truth of the situation. Yes, some humans decide to stay at the end of seven years, but it's a small percentage of them. I'm too smart to bet on such unlikely odds.

I don't even know what I'm worried about. I've had partners and relationships and even love a time or two. It's always faded. Interest wanders. Ambition rises. Circumstances change. That's been true 100 percent of the time. It will be true this time, too.

We'll be sick of each other within a year. She'll have some fun with anyone who catches her eye. I'll get back to my climb up the political ladder until I secure the spot of Azazel's second-in-command. Simpler that way.

So why does the thought bother me so much?

CHAPTER 7

LENORA

Having sex with the demon who wants me to bargain seven years of my life isn't exactly a high point in my life. I'd love to say sex is just sex and isn't enough to make me act foolish, but I'm in this situation to begin with because sex made me act foolish. It's not a comforting thought.

I shower Ramanu off me and take a few extra minutes to clean the blood from beneath my nails. Even now, little shivers of pleasure keep working their way through me. Damn them, but that was *good*.

Usually sex is one thing or another. A battle of wills or a soft landing. It's never been a strange combination of both. Not that there's anything *soft* about what happened with Ramanu. But there's trust to ease the sexy back-and-forth I enjoy so much, and I'd be a liar if I said I didn't relish the way they held me afterward. A bonding moment I can't afford to let muddy my mind but that I craved far more than I should have. I felt cared for, and even if it's a lie, it makes my chest twinge uncomfortably.

I walk to the bathroom door and wince. They aren't small,

and they weren't particularly gentle—fine in the moment, but I can hardly be walking funny through the market.

Ramanu is sitting on the bed when I come back into the bedroom. It's freshly made and perfectly clean. There's an honest-to-gods gift basket sitting on the dresser. Of course there is. I inhale deeply. "Brownie magic." It's got a distinctive scent, though they're relatively rare these days. The competition to entice them into partnership is fierce.

"Yes." Ramanu's mouth turns down. "You're hurt."

"I'm fine." It's an effort to keep my stride relatively smooth as I walk to my bag.

"I should have thought to bring some balm..." Ramanu sniffs. "What do you have there?"

I finish untwisting the cap on the balm I just pulled from my bag and laugh. "Come now. Where do you think bargainer demons get that balm from? We're the ones who taught you to make it." Or so the legend goes. I'm sure reality is far less romantic than a witch falling in love with a bargainer demon and dreaming up a healing balm so they could go at it like rabbits, day in and day out.

Either way, it's a useful tool to have on hand, especially for events where I plan to fuck my way through the next three days. Granted, I packed it mostly out of habit. This Shadow Market is different than the last few. It's not all fun and games.

I desperately need to get my amulet back.

Ramanu plucks the container from my hand. "Allow me."

I give them a long look. "I'm more than capable of doing it myself." Even as I say it, my body thrums with remembered pleasure. It was good with them. Too good. *Distractingly* good.

I've gone down that route before and look where I ended up. Fucked, and not in a good way. "Ramanu—"

"We won't get distracted," they cut in smoothly. "You have places to be, after all."

KATEE ROBERT

I shouldn't. But even as I think it, I find myself backing to the edge of the bed and sinking onto it. Ramanu comes to kneel in front of me and gently guides my legs wide. Their claws retract with a quiet *snick.*

"Neat trick," I manage.

"It has its purposes." They dip their fingers into the balm. It's almost unbearably intimate to watch them press those fingers into me. The relief is nearly instantaneous. The balm can't heal major wounds, but it's great for little wear-and-tear things like rough fucking.

Ramanu lingers a little longer than strictly necessary, gently fucking me with their fingers. They sigh. "I promised, but you're a tempting little thing, Lenora. I could play with you for eternity."

Eternity is a whole lot longer than seven years, which I still haven't agreed to. Will *not* agree to.

Pleasure starts building, but Ramanu eases their fingers out of me before it gets too overwhelming. I clench the comforter to keep from grabbing their hand and shoving it back between my legs. I'm here for a reason. I cannot forget that.

To distract myself, I blurt the first thing that comes into my mind. "Why do you have the double set of horns? Most bargainers don't." Not that I have a lot of direct experience with their people, but my family keeps detailed records going back generations. Great-grandmother isn't the only one who summoned a demon; she's just the only one who did it multiple times and left such specific notes after the fact.

Ramanu shakes their head. "Rude, aren't you?"

I flush when I realize how that would sound if I asked a human why their body is a certain way. "Gods, I'm sorry. Forget I said anything. I'm a bitch, but I'm not usually careless."

"It's fine." They smirk. "I have a double set of horns for

52

the same reason I can see magic and emotions. My parent is a gargoyle. My mother is a bargainer demon. It makes for interesting family gatherings." They tap the horns coming out of their eye sockets. "Bargainers have a habit of playing with a wide variety of partners, and sometimes children result from those unions. Those children often have...quirks...as a result."

"Oh," I say faintly.

"And you..." They lean in and inhale deeply. "One of your ancestors was brave indeed. No wonder you have access to a celestial amulet of protection. The thread of your blood is faint, but even faint, it's nearly overpowering."

I blink. "What are you talking about?"

"Celestial." They grin. "Apparently that distant ancestor of yours was *very* loved by that god."

I don't know what to do with that information. It doesn't really change anything. It's common knowledge that humans don't have power on their own but that they're great conductors for *others'* powers through procreating. By that understanding, it's not out of the realm of belief that all witches have paranormal blood in their family history.

But *celestial*?

Is it possible the amulet is just a protection spell and the real power comes from the *celestial* blood in our veins? The thought is staggering. I shake my head slowly. I can't afford to believe it or doubt what I've always been told. The cost is too high for being wrong. "Even with all that, I can't get the amulet back from Kristoff."

"His family is more intentional with their lines." Ramanu moves back almost reluctantly and starts to dress. I mourn the sight of their body being covered with clothing, even as I appreciate them keeping me on task.

I don't like what it says about me that fucking is enough to derail my focus. Apparently I haven't learned my lesson after all. I grab my dress from the ground and pull it on. A few minutes in the bathroom to fix my hair and makeup as much as possible, and then there's nothing left to stall with.

What am I saying? I'm not stalling. I'm ready to kill this motherfucker.

Ramanu is lounging on the bed when I leave the bathroom. "Do you have a plan?"

"Kill Kristoff. Take the amulet. Not in that order." The amulet is protecting him, which means I need to remove it first. The problem is that he won't let me—or anyone else— get close enough to do it. "Jack's going to try to take the amulet during the event tonight."

"Jack," Ramanu says slowly.

"Yes. They're good with their hands, and I trust them to give it back to me." Jack doesn't need the amulet to protect them. After we decided we were better off as friends, they fell in with a werewolf who's downright feral for them. I'm honestly surprised that Skye wasn't hovering at their shoulder in the market earlier. She usually doesn't let them out of her sight.

Jack doesn't know about the amulet being the source of my family's power, but *no one* knows about that. I'd like to say that wouldn't make a difference in their helping me, but I've never trusted someone enough to tell them that particular secret. I'm not about to start now, when it matters the most.

Ramanu pushes slowly to their feet. "A long shot of a plan."

Frustration flares, but I ignore it. They aren't wrong, but that doesn't mean I'm about to admit it. "You would say that, seeing as you want me to make a bargain with you."

"I'm serious, Lenora." For once, their lightly mocking tone is nowhere in evidence. "Kristoff is protected. You and your friends aren't."

I hate the reminder as much as I hate the reality of this situation. "Yes, I'm aware. But all Jack has to do is grab the amulet and get to Sanctuary." Not even Kristoff can harm them there, and if he's so busy chasing after Jack, I'll have a chance to slip a knife between his ribs. As long as I do it before *he* reaches Sanctuary. It's a designated neutral zone, and it's magically enforced."

"Hmmm." Ramanu opens the door and holds it for me. "And me as your fail-safe."

"I won't need you." But even as I say it, I wonder. Our plan is a decent one. The event tonight will be crowded, and everyone will be drinking and partying. It's practically tradition to steal shit from each other and then hook up in the shadows, to the point where you don't bring anything to the event you're *not* willing to part with. Another way we magical beings show our prowess over each other.

Games. Always games.

I used to love it. I've never been great at pickpocketing or sleight of hand, but the rush of catching someone trying to take crystals from my pockets and the rush of what came after... It made me feel alive.

Now I'm just tired. Jack doesn't play like that anymore now that they've settled down. Olivia sticks to the family-friendly events here with her girlfriend and kids. The only person who will be there to party tonight is *Kristoff*, and if that's not depressing, I don't know what is.

Ramanu stops next to me as I step out onto the street. "Something wrong, little witch?"

I don't even consider lying or brushing them off. I just answer honestly. "I'm a dark witch. Dark witches aren't supposed to get sad because all their exes are off living their best lives. We aren't supposed to get tired of the fighting and fucking and theatrics." But I *am* tired. I never realized how much until this mess with Kristoff.

"Lenora." Ramanu catches my wrist lightly. "This isn't about the amulet."

KATEE ROBERT

"No, I guess it isn't." I sigh. "Look, it's nothing. Just one of those things where you get older and look around and realize everyone around you has settled down yet you're still living like you're twenty. Most of the time, it doesn't bother me." Much.

But the times when it does?

It makes me wonder what's wrong with me that I can't have what my fathers have. A love—an *acceptance*—that goes soul deep. All my exes have tried to change me or have found me wanting. It's the nature of the beast. There's a reason they're exes, even the ones I've maintained friendships with. We didn't match.

In my darkest moments, I wonder if there's anyone who actually matches me.

Ramanu falls into step next to me, easily matching their longer stride to my shorter one. We move through the streets toward the main market area. It's just come into sight when Ramanu catches my arm. "Lenora."

I like the way they say my name. I like it entirely too much. The pet name is cute, but their voice goes low and serious when they use my actual name. I can't believe I was so reckless as to sleep with them. It's going to be Kristoff all over again, except this time the stakes are even higher. "I can't do this."

"Lenora," they repeat. They don't release me, but I'm not exactly trying to jerk my arm free. I just stand there and look up at them helplessly. Ramanu squeezes my arm gently. "We'll get the amulet back. I promise. You don't have to worry."

"The cost is too high," I whisper. I *like* Ramanu. Even with the bickering—maybe *especially* with the bickering—it's been a really enjoyable day. If the circumstances were different...but they aren't.

They curse softly and drop their hand from my arm. "Goddess save me, but Azazel is going to kick my ass."

"What?"

"We'll get the amulet back," they repeat. They shake their head. "Not as a bargain. We can discuss that later."

I stare. Surely they're not saying what I think they're saying. "Ramanu, the whole reason you're here is to get those seven years from me."

"Yeah." They shrug. "But I like to color outside the lines and piss my leader off sometimes. This will just be one added to the list."

They just lied to me. I'm certain of it. If what they said earlier was true about the celestial blood, I imagine making a bargain with me would be a coup. I don't entirely understand how bargainer magic works, but obviously there's something about the bargain itself that is powerful and fundamental to their magic. They aren't just hauling over humans to breed with and add half-demon babies to their ranks; if they were, then children would be part of the contract rather than a caveat *if* it happens.

Ramanu is ambitious. I can practically taste their striving on my tongue. Yes, I summoned them, but I believe them when they say they had their attention on me before that moment. They went after me because I'd be a feather in their cap. They have absolutely no motivation to offer to help without a deal attached. "Ramanu—"

"Let's stop wasting time. We're headed this way?" They start walking before I have a chance to respond, easily weaving through the crowds starting to gather for the night's activities. I curse under my breath and scramble after them. Through it all, I can't help feeling I've missed something important.

CHAPTER 8

RAMANU

I am a fool. It's the only explanation I can come up with for why I've thrown all my plans out the window because a little human witch turned baby blue with enough strength for me to see the lost look in her eyes. I don't like my witch being sad, let alone experiencing bone-deep sorrow when she thinks about her life.

I want to bathe her in sunny yellow and deep ocean blue, to keep her happy and content always.

Fool.

I can practically hear Azazel's voice in the back of my mind, but he's not one to talk. He's lost his head over a human, too. And now the entire castle is watching them circle each other warily like our leader isn't wearing his heart on his sleeve every time he's in the room with her. For her part, Eve seems to want nothing more than to avoid him for the next seven years.

Will that be my fate? To follow this snappy little witch around like a lost puppy while all my peers chuckle at my antics?

The thought should make me more uncomfortable than it

does. It certainly shouldn't leave a strange warmth in my chest. Lenora would give me a run for my money, and she's already proven she's vicious when provoked...and surprisingly sweet when she's naked and coming. I like the sweetness with my spice. A lot.

I like *her*.

But then, I knew that, didn't I?

Lenora catches up to me, and I slow to match her pace. Her magic shifts and changes from minute to minute. She doesn't know what to think of my offer, but that's fine. I don't really know what to think of it, either.

I knew I wanted to keep her, but this is impulsive in the extreme. Somewhere, no doubt, Sol is laughing at me in that dragon way of his. Comeuppance is a very human thing to believe in, but I'm experiencing a bit of it right now.

Lenora leads the way through a series of tight walkways to a large open area where the ceiling arches so high, it's lost in the shadows. The party has already started. People are gathered in a sickly swirl of color, drinking and laughing. More than a few of them are fucking, both on the dance floor and in the shallow alcoves that circle the space. Not quite out of sight but close enough that the illusion of privacy is maintained.

I expect the little witch to relax into the mood—she said this used to be a thing she enjoyed—but the exact opposite happens. If anything, her shoulders inch higher and she seems to draw in on herself.

She also moves a little closer to me.

I don't think she realizes she's done it. It's barely a half step in my direction, almost more of a lean. I clock it, though. I'm too attuned to her not to. Something in my chest takes a sickening dip in response. I hold perfectly still to resist the urge to put my arms around her, to turn and put my body between her and the rest of these people.

Her color goes a sickly yellow green, and I tense. I follow

her attention to where a man bathed in bright pink and the deep yellow of amusement has just entered the space across from us. I can taste his magic from here, a thread of many notes and as distinctive as Lenora's. Between that and the bright white globe radiating from where it hangs around his neck, he's instantly identifiable.

Kristoff.

He turns in our direction, and his amusement deepens, along with a surge of rich green jealousy as he takes me in and how close we're standing. Cute. Apparently he's feeling possessive of my witch. I already planned on ripping out the bastard's throat for making Lenora sad and scared, but his jealousy makes me want to kill him slowly.

She trusted him, let him close enough to steal the amulet that kept her *safe*, and now he's parading that trust where anyone can see. He's making it something to be ashamed of, when I'd give one of my horns to have Lenora trust me like that.

It's not a comfortable thought, but nothing about this is comfortable.

"Lenora." I wait for her to acknowledge me to continue in a low voice, "If Jack is doing the lift, then standing here and staring is going to draw attention."

"Right." She drags in a rough breath. "Yes. Okay. We should..."

I am not a good person. I enjoy creating chaos entirely too much to be labeled something as sweet as *good*. Even as I speak, I tell myself the last thing this situation needs is for me to stir the pot. "He's jealous."

Shock ripples through her. "Excuse me?"

"I can see it clearly. Jealousy is a rich green. Very pretty color. Very distinctive. When he looks at us, he's rife with it."

"Why are you telling me this?" she asks in a low voice. "I

couldn't give a damn if that motherfucker is jealous. He doesn't have a claim on me. He never did."

She needs the distraction as much as the situation does. If she weren't so affected by this asshole, she would have thought of it herself. It makes me want to bundle her up and take her somewhere safe where I can fuck the worry right out of her head like I did earlier today then return here and rip Kristoff's head clean off. I bet there's a spike somewhere around here I could stick it on. A clear warning not to cross my witch.

Dangerous thoughts.

"Distraction." I land on the word and cling to it. There's a purpose to this, and it's not simply because I want Lenora in my arms again. "We need to give Jack a distraction to work with."

"That's a terrible idea."

"Is it?" I lean down until our faces are nearly even. In the corner of my senses, Kristoff's jealousy nearly eclipses the rest of the room. "He's not looking anywhere but at us right now. He's not thinking about who might be coming up behind him to slip that amulet off his neck."

Lenora laughs. "You sure you're not just trying to get back in my pants?"

"I would like to live in your pants." I keep talking before she can do more than make a choked sound. "But while I'm not opposed to an audience, I hardly think this is the situation to indulge."

"I see." She sounds so shocked, I want to kiss her.

In fact... "Let me kiss you, little witch. Let's give them a show." When she hesitates, I find myself continuing. "You can let go with me. I'll keep you safe."

"Then who will keep *you* safe?"

Goddess, but I like this witch. I smile. "You, of course. Who else?"

She doesn't respond with words. She simply slides her

hands up my chest and around my neck. I lift her, and Lenora wraps her legs around my waist.

It's tempting to simply take her mouth now. But I want to taste my witch, to enjoy this first. I shift my grip to her thighs and ease her up a bit higher. It's the most natural thing in the world to slip my hands up the slits on either side of her dress and grip her ass. She jerks against me. "*Ramanu.*"

"L—"

Lenora kisses me. Of course she does. She's not one to wait for the other person to make a move, not when the path is clear and she has her eye on what she wants. What my witch wants is my mouth. Her magic sparks against my tongue, bright and near-painful.

I don't decide to walk us to the nearest wall and pin her against it. My body simply takes over. For all my determination not to fuck her right here where we'd both be defenseless, I'm suddenly not quite sure why it's such a terrible idea.

Her lust is bright enough that I can't see anyone but her. Dangerous, that, but I don't give a fuck. I can protect her from anyone here, not that she needs my protection. I'll bathe the room with their blood if they think to so much as touch her without permission. I have a feeling she'd do the same for those she cares about. The thought has me pulling her closer. I can *scent* her need, am overwhelmed with the desire to fulfill it.

I transfer her weight to one hand and then shift the grip of my other, angling so I can stroke her clit with my thumb. She flares brighter in response. Lenora sets her teeth against my bottom lip. Not quite a bite, but I nearly cum in my pants in response.

She kisses along my jaw to my ear. "Bad demon, making me so wet in front of all these people."

My chuckle comes out strained. "Guess I better get you off to make up for it."

"Do it," she breathes.

Green starts to edge into the pink haze Lenora's lust has created. I turn my head and growl. "He's coming over here." I make myself stop stroking her pussy. "Do you want me to put you down?"

"No." She digs her nails into my shoulders. "Don't stop, either." Lenora drags in a breath. "That is, if you're okay with fingering me in front of my ex."

As if I wouldn't happily do much more to stake the claim I certainly do not have on this witch. I retract my claws and press two fingers into her. "I'm okay with it."

"*Oh*." Her head falls back to rest against the wall, and I take advantage of the position to drag my mouth over her throat. Lenora makes that delicious little whimper. "Good. Ah. That's good."

The green is now close enough that I can feel Kristoff's movement as he comes up and leans against the wall next to us. "Interesting choice, Lenora."

"Kristoff." She rolls her hips as I fuck her slowly with my fingers, but most of my attention is on the man next to us. I lean a little harder on her against the wall, freeing one hand in case I need to disembowel him. Except I can't do that, can I? Lenora has a plan, and it doesn't include me killing Kristoff. Overriding her will is the wrong call, even if I were able to get the amulet back as a result.

We have to do this her way.

He snorts. "You've made your point, though I didn't peg you as desperate enough to make a bargain and give up seven years of your life...let alone fuck the bargainer demon." He tsks. "Your taste really is abominable."

She tenses, and I press my thumb to her clit, circling slowly. It's tempting to snarl at Kristoff, but my witch doesn't need me to fight her battles. Sure enough, she gives a lazy laugh. "Baby, if you're jealous, just say so. Give me back my amulet, and I'll consider letting you take me out again." She gasps when I wedge a third finger into her. "If Ramanu ever leaves me wanting, that is."

"Ramanu." He says my name as if it tastes foul in his mouth. "Have fun with her, demon."

I'm going to have fun choking you to death with your own entrails.

I should grin. Should make some smart comment like I normally do. Instead, I snarl. "She's not interested. You're interrupting. Fuck off."

His rich green dips into the sickly yellow green of hate. The feeling is entirely mutual. I turn back to Lenora, though I continue to monitor Kristoff as he huffs and moves away from us.

"Ramanu." Lenora's voice is thick with something that isn't lust. Colors swirl through her, nearly too fast to follow. She doesn't know how to feel, and strangely enough, I'm in the same place.

I'm not a particularly peaceful person, but I normally don't jump straight to a nearly overwhelming desire to murder someone I just met. Kristoff shows all evidence of being a giant asshole of a human, but he's just that...a human. Even with all his magic and bloodlines, there's nothing he could do to save himself from me.

That is, if he didn't have the amulet protecting him.

"*Ramanu.*"

I allow her hand on my neck to urge me down, and I carefully brush a kiss to her lips. Her nails dig into my skin. "Make me cum, and let's get out of here."

She doesn't have to tell me twice. The temptation to tease this out is there, but I don't like having my back to this room. So far, the energy is all fun with a kind of reckless abandon that makes me think it could turn into a violent mob or an orgy, depending on what inciting incident there is.

I kiss Lenora properly as I start working her with my

fingers again. She clings to me with the desperation of a sailor holding the last piece of shipwreck to stay afloat. There's no reason for that to feel like it means something.

For her, this is just a distraction. A good time. A *taste test* she has no intention of buying the full experience for.

But, as she orgasms hard enough that her nails draw blood on my neck, I can't shake the feeling that she's marked me in a vastly more permanent way.

CHAPTER 9

LENORA

I know Jack failed the moment I see their face. Ramanu and I have been posted up at a little table right on the edge of Sanctuary, easily able to jump across the boundary if needed. Turns out it's not necessary.

Jack drops into the chair across from us and sighs. A light sheen of sweat coats their medium-brown skin. "Sorry. I tried. He's in the middle of a godsdamned threesome. I couldn't get through." They fan themself with a hand. "Gods, I'm nervous sweating. This is ridiculous."

"He almost caught them." Skye appears behind them. She's a lean white woman with a shaved head and a nose ring. Her shirt looks like she clawed off the arms and lower part, showcasing a set of abs that looks painted on. She's not pretty, exactly, but there's an energy around her that draws people in. "I was going to have to step in."

When Skye steps in, blood flows. It's what I like about her.

Unfortunately, her brand of frenzied violence wouldn't help us at all in this situation. "If Jack couldn't get to him, I think Kristoff would have had time to throw up a shield if he saw you coming." Subtlety and Skye don't go well together.

"Pity," Ramanu murmurs.

Jack gives them a long look before turning to me. "I'm sorry this didn't work."

"It's okay." I sigh. "It was a long shot anyways. Kristoff is too clever to allow it to be lifted off him, but we had to try."

Ramanu shifts and drapes an arm over the back of my chair. They're barely touching me, but I like it far more than I should. It's hard not to lean back into the comforting weight of them. I know better. Damn it, *I do*.

The demon wants something from me.

They wouldn't still be here if they didn't. They certainly wouldn't be helping me.

Except...they seem genuinely worried about me. I move on instinct, shifting closer and squeezing their knee. "It's okay. There's another way."

"What other way?" they ask softly.

The one thing I wanted to avoid. I close my eyes and inhale deeply. "We have to enter the tournament tomorrow."

Jack's eyes go wide. "That's a fool's bargain."

"I know."

They shake their head. "Len, he's got the amulet. He's a surefire winner. No one is going to get close enough touch him. And he's *pissed* at you right now. He'll wipe the floor with you and then laugh his way out of the ring."

"I *know*." I can't even be mad at their estimation because it's exactly what will happen. Magic won't affect him, and while Kristoff isn't exactly a warrior, I have to get close enough to strike. If he's using offensive magic—and he will—then I won't get a chance. "But he can't come into the ring with spells in place, so if I can get to him before he throws up the shield to keep me from taking the amulet, then I have a shot."

Skye snorts. "A long shot. The longest."

"Thank you, Skye. I am well aware of the odds."

Ramanu has been surveying us silently. Their thumb

brushes my shoulder. It's not a sexual touch. It's almost like they're trying to comfort me. I give their knee another squeeze and they spare a brief smile. "Explain the tournament."

Jack's the one who leans forward, their curls bouncing with the movement. "Exactly what you'd expect. Two people enter the ring, winner is the one who beats the other to a pulp. Sometimes murder happens. Anything goes, though as Len says, you can't walk into the ring with spells in place."

"The amulet doesn't count as a spell?"

I allow myself to lean back against their arm, and they respond by tugging my chair closer to them so they can wrap their arm around my shoulders properly. It feels nice. Really nice. I clear my throat. "It's a loophole."

They study me. "Have you entered the tournament using that loophole before?"

My skin heats, even though I'm certain I have no reason to be embarrassed. "Only once. When I was nineteen." Afterward, my fathers found out and gave me a blistering hour-long lecture about misusing the powers of the amulet. My Byrne dad, in particular, was displeased about me using the family heirloom in such a way.

It's for personal protection, Lenora. Not *for personal gain.*

"Did you win?"

"Of course she won." Jack snorts. "Cleaned up. She even kicked Skye's ass."

Skye lifts her top lip in a snarl. "I don't like loopholes." She jumps when Jack nudges her. "But no hard feelings about the broken back."

"Broken back," Ramanu echoes.

I tense. I had nearly this exact conversation with Jack and Skye the first time I introduced them to Olivia. She'd been horrified by the violence. Up until that point, my dark magic was mostly in theory for her. Hearing Jack and Skye cackle about the damage I'd done in the ring...

We didn't last another month before she sat me down and gently broke things off. Her girlfriend is a midwife and hobby baker; the only thing she punches is dough to make mouthwatering bread.

I lift my chin. I'm not going to apologize for who I am. I'm done with that. If that means I end up alone because the only people who like spending time with witches who use dark magic are other witches who use dark magic and there's a thread that runs through all of us.

We aren't trustworthy. Not with each other, at least. Maybe not at all.

"Efficient," Ramanu says.

Skye gives a toothy grin. "Isn't it? She pulverized my spine with a spell. Took a few hours to heal."

Jack laughs. "To be fair, you were trying to claw her to ribbons."

"Nature of the beast." Skye snorts. "Get it. The beast. It's me."

They giggle like a bunch of schoolkids at the ridiculous pun. I can't quite relax. I glance at Ramanu, only to find their lips curved. I frown. "Why are you smiling? They're talking about me *pulverizing* Skye's spine."

"Skye's fine and obviously harbors no hard feelings. Why would it bother me?" Their smile doesn't dim. "You're a fearsome little thing, aren't you?"

I narrow my eyes. "What's that supposed to mean?"

"You don't need me to protect you. You're more than capable of protecting both of us." They lean down until their front horns brush my temple, lowering their voice so they're speaking just for me. "It's okay, Lenora. You don't have to fight this time. I said I'll take care of it, and I will."

The temptation to let them do it is nearly overwhelming. If anyone can pull it off, it's Ramanu, a bargainer demon. But if I do that, then *they'll* have the amulet. The thought leaves my stomach in tangles. "And then you'll force me to bargain for the amulet back." They've been nothing but honest about their aims, and with that as leverage, they'd have a clear path to get what they want.

"That would be the smart thing to do." They say it strangely, though. They brush a kiss to my temple and sit back. "Can anyone enter the tournament?"

"Yeah, you just show up early enough to put your name in." Jack leans back against Skye. "I'm starving. Let's go get something to eat." They look back at me. "Let me know if there's anything we can do to help."

Jack has quick fingers, but they aren't a fighter, and if Skye couldn't beat me with the amulet, she's certainly not going to beat Kristoff. I force a smile even though my shoulders feel so tight, they're wound up to my ears. "Thank you for trying tonight. Enjoy the rest of Samhain."

Skye laces her fingers through Jack's and pulls them to their feet. "Oh, we plan on it. See you around." She tows Jack into the thinning crowd.

The Shadow Market runs mostly nonstop from midnight of the opening ceremony until the closing ceremony. There are definitely peak hours, but the crowds fluctuate throughout. Right now is a relatively low time, but it won't last long.

I allow myself to lean my head back against Ramanu's arm for a ten count. When I get to the end, I lift my head and push to my feet. I offer Ramanu my hand. Not because they need help getting out of the chair. More because I want an excuse to keep up the contact with them. "We might as well grab some food and get some rest. We won't have another chance tonight."

If I slept with Kristoff again, I might be able to get the amulet.

The thought makes my skin crawl. I can't do it. Not after he betrayed me so thoroughly. He left me without my protection, but more: he knows he took a family heirloom that's been passed down for generations. It's priceless and irreplaceable, and if he cared about me even a little, he wouldn't have done it.

I...can't do it.

"What are you thinking?"

Once again, I don't consider lying. "If I fucked Kristoff, I might be able to distract him enough to get the amulet." I don't really believe it, though. He'll be waiting for me to try something. The more likely outcome is that he'll use me for orgasms the same way he used me to get the amulet, and then he'll leave me with only shame and regret for company.

Ramanu goes tense. "No. Out of the question."

I agree with them, but that doesn't stop me from raising my eyebrows. "Sorry, but did you think you get a say about who I fuck or why?"

"Not yet."

I blink. "What do you mean 'not yet'?"

They lace their fingers through mine without answering. I don't like that. I don't like it at all. But what am I supposed to do? I need them as a fail-safe, and we both know it. I reluctantly lead them away from Sanctuary, heading toward the food stalls.

I've never felt as conflicted as I am around Ramanu. I like the demon, and I *really* like how we fuck, but out of everyone I've ever been with, their agenda is the clearest.

Seven years of my life.

I can't forget that, and while I appreciate that they've been very up front about their goals, that doesn't change the fact it's a sword hanging over my neck. I don't know if I can beat Kristoff. The cost of failure just seems to compound the longer he has the amulet.

I'm scared by how much I want to ask Ramanu to handle it for me.

They stop unexpectedly, I make it several steps before our linked hands pull me up short. I turn back. "What's wrong?"

"Stop that."

"Stop what?"

"You don't have to do this alone. Stop being so stubborn and let me help you."

I release their hands and cross my arms over my chest. "I *hate* that you can read my emotions or mind or scent or whatever you're doing." In the past I've prided myself on my poker face, on not letting anyone close.

Maybe that's part of the problem.

I shove the words away. I've made my choices, and I don't regret them. Mostly. I don't need Ramanu poking around inside my head, even if that's not what they're actually doing. I have good shields. They couldn't if they tried. It's still incredibly uncomfortable to be *seen* so clearly no matter what my face is doing. I swallow hard. "Stop it."

"No."

I blink. "Excuse me?"

"No. It's a simple word, little witch." They shift closer but make no move to touch me. "It's part of who I am, the same way your magic is part of you. Even if I could shut it off, I wouldn't."

I open my mouth to argue and then stop short. I'm lashing out at Ramanu because I'm angry about the situation. Before now, I don't know if I'd have realized it or been able to put on the brakes even if I had. I manage to grit my teeth and say, "Then at least stop commenting on it all the time. It's invasive."

"It's really not." An edge creeps into Ramanu's voice. "You're splashing your emotions out for everyone to see. It's not my fault no one else bothers to look closely enough to see them." They grip my shoulders lightly. "*Let me help you, Lenora.* You don't have to do this alone."

Again, that horrible wavering feeling rises inside me. I want to say yes. I want it so badly, I'm about to start shaking. It's been weeks of fear and panic, trying to get that amulet back from Kristoff. Even asking Jack for help wasn't easy, but at least I knew Jack wouldn't hold it against me. That's not how they roll.

I don't have that assurance with Ramanu. In fact, I have the exact opposite.

"I do have to," I whisper.

"No, you don't." Their jaw goes tight. "I'll enter the ring and take back the amulet."

"For the cost of seven years."

They mutter something that sounds like a curse. "No."

"Don't lie to me."

"I'm not." They drop their hands. "I like you, little witch. And I've developed an instant dislike for that particular ex of yours. I'll do this because I want to."

I want to believe them. I really, really do. But if I've learned one thing, it's that if something seems too good to be true, it almost definitely is. "I can't trust you." It scares me how badly I want to trust them. That feeling has only ever betrayed me in the past. Surely this time won't be any different. I can't risk it. Not when the stakes are so high.

That's not the full truth, though, is it? "I don't want you hurt, Ramanu. Not because you're trying to help me." Demon or no, the fact is Kristoff is formidable. Maybe Ramanu will win, but I can't imagine it will be a costless victory. The thought of them being hurt because of me makes my stomach twist. "Don't ask me again. I made this mess. I'll be the one to clean it up."

They make a sound of frustration. "If you won't allow me to help with the tournament, what *will* you allow?"

I should say nothing. The smartest thing would be to cut ties now. Ramanu can find their way back to their realm without me doing a formal banishment; they come and go as they please when not summoned, and there's no reason they can't do exactly that right now. There's not a single reason I can't walk away from them now.

Except...I don't want to.

"We can't do anything until the tournament. Could you..." Gods, what am I about to do? I push forward before common sense can pump the brakes. "Can you keep me distracted until it's time?"

CHAPTER 10

RAMANU

I really must be as perverse as Azazel laughingly calls me, because there's no other explanation for me falling for this difficult, stubborn witch. Given enough time, I have no doubt she'd figure out a way to take that amulet back from the bastard. No one can keep their guard up indefinitely, and in a few years, Kristoff would turn a corner and there Lenora would be. Ready to strike.

But that would mean admitting to her fathers that she lost it, and that's one thing my witch won't do. Instead, she's getting desperate. Desperation is what drives humans to bargain. Desperation makes them sloppy and reckless.

Desperation can get someone killed.

The thought makes me want to snarl, but Lenora will take it as me snarling at *her*, and then her walls will come up further. I know she wants to send me away. It's written right there where anyone like me can see it. She doesn't trust me, and I can't blame her for that.

Except she trusts me enough to put her body in my hands. It would be so easy to look into that, to fall victim to my own fantasy. The truth is much harsher.

Lenora might guard her heart with spikes and blades and high walls, but she's startlingly reckless when it comes to her body. I don't judge her for her past partners or her reasons for being with them, but the urge to bundle her up and keep her safe rises again, stronger than before.

Yes, I'm falling for this witch. I think it started even before I met her.

If there's some vengeful force out there, it's laughing uproariously about the fact I've so enjoyed needling that damned mate-stricken dragon and now I'm following this murderous little witch around as if attached to a leash.

We pause long enough to grab some food from one of the carts and then head back to the room. I close the door softly and turn toward her, intent on continuing our earlier argument. If she'd just let me *help* her...

Lenora drops her dress. She looks over her shoulder at me. "I'm going to take a shower." Without another word, she strips off her boots and walks into the bathroom.

She leaves the door open.

It's a clear invitation, and I find myself following even as I try to reason through why continuing to fuck her is a terrible idea. It's taboo in the extreme, but I've already crossed that line, so doing it again won't make a difference. She's feeling vulnerable and off-center and using sex to keep those uncomfortable emotions at bay, but I've already decided not to use it against her, to offer her a safe space amid this storm. She thinks I'm trying to fuck her into agreeing to the bargain, and there's not much I can do about that assumption. In the past, I would have used every tool in my arsenal *except* sex to close the bargain.

Now I'm not certain I'd take the deal even if she offered it. It doesn't feel good. I want her to come to me because she wants to, not because she's backed into a corner and can't see a way out.

She asked for a distraction, though. It's the only thing she asked of me. If I'm not willing to do this, surely she won't trust me enough to ask for more. Except that reasoning doesn't quite make the conflicted feeling inside me ease. I want to keep her safe, and I can't tell if fucking me will offer the distraction she needs...or be the blade she turns on herself in punishment.

I duck my head to clear the door and find Lenora stepping into a steaming spray of water. The bathroom is bigger than I expected, the shower tiled and plenty large enough for both of us.

Lenora turns to face me. Pink rises within her, but it's tempered with red and gray. She wants me, wants this, but she's still angry at my perceived intrusion of reading her emotions, and she's worried about a number of things.

I won't accept this bargain; Lenora will be a fish that escapes my net at the end of Samhain. Honestly, I should leave her to it. She's smart and ruthless and fully capable of saving herself. The longer I stay here, the more I risk giving my heart to a witch who doesn't want it and won't thank me for the offering.

I always thought it was funny to watch my peers fall for their partners. To see them go sappy and lovestruck. I never experienced it on this level, never forgot myself and my aims so completely.

"You trusted Jack to help you." I don't know why I speak. I can't help the edge of jealousy that works its way into my tone. "Trust me to help you."

Lenora laughs harshly. "I've known Jack since I was eighteen and filled with more hormones than sense. We've had our ups and downs, but Jack has more than earned my trust in that time. I've only known you a single day, and I don't care what reconnaissance you've done on me or what you think you know about me... You don't."

"Lenora—"

"And even as much as I trust Jack, they don't know—" She stops short.

It's too late. She slipped up. I narrow my attention on her. "They don't know *what*, little witch?" But even as I ask, little inconsistencies click into place. Lenora obviously loves her fathers, but she doesn't fear them. Losing this family heirloom might get her a lecture, but Lenora is who she is—she's obviously received plenty over the years. That isn't enough to cause this level of desperation. "An amulet from a celestial to their human lover..."

"Ramanu, please," she whispers.

"It's not just protection that it offers, is it?" She turns a gray so light, it's nearly white. She's *terrified*. It's almost enough to make me stop, but I need to know the truth. I press onward. "How much of your family's magic is linked to that amulet?"

"Damn you."

It's all the confirmation I need. What I'm not prepared for is the fear that lances through me. "Kristoff has had it for weeks."

"Yes."

"If your magic hasn't started drying up already, it could do so at any time."

Lenora slumps back against the shower wall. "Yes."

Without the amulet boosting her magic, she'll be significantly weaker. Not defenseless, no, but near to it. "You can't enter the tournament." Even if she can somehow get the amulet off Kristoff's neck, she might not have her magic at her disposal. He could still kill her, could snuff out the life I'm coming to value so highly. "Kristoff could kill you."

"It's possible." She sounds so tired. "But it's the only way."

"Lenora—"

She sighs. "I like you, Ramanu. I won't pretend I don't. But that doesn't mean I'll trust you with more than my body. Especially now that you know the truth about the amulet."

One of the first things a bargainer demon is taught is when to cut and run. Not all bargains go through. Even when we do our due diligence and pick targets primed to say yes, it doesn't always work out. Due to the quirk of my gargoyle heritage, I've failed less often than most.

I'm not going to get Lenora to say yes to me.

Not about any of this. Not the bargain. Not the help.

Frustration wraps a fist around my throat and squeezes. "You can't do this alone."

"I suppose we'll see." Her fear fades to a sorrowful pale blue. "We're talking in circles, Ramanu. I understand if you're leaving—no hard feelings—but if you're staying, take off your clothes and get in here."

I should leave. It's the smart thing to do. I've never had my heart broken, and it seems ridiculous in the extreme that a little human witch can grind it to dust, but there's no denying the pressure in my chest. Or the source.

I must have some of that masochistic streak Azazel claims I do, though, because I shut the bathroom door and yank off my shirt. If this is the only way she'll let me take care of her, then so be it.

My boots and pants follow, and I step through the gap in the tiled wall to join Lenora in the shower. The steam feels good on my skin. I had barely registered the faint chill of the market, but it melts away instantly.

I touch the glass bottles carefully arranged on a shelf on the wall, the magic infused in the labels identifying them. Shampoo. Conditioner. Bodywash. Lube. The last makes me chuckle a little despite my dark mood. "This place is truly prepared for everything, isn't it?"

"Yes."

I want to chase away the fear still lingering in her. "Play your cards right, and I'll let you peg me."

Shock flares, followed by a pink so intense, I clearly see her features. "If that's an honest offer, I'm saying hell yes."

"Then be a good little witch and let me take care of you." I've never been overly interested in the pampering of humans. It always seemed like a waste of time. I ensure my contracted humans have everything they need and are protected, but indulging in the little things was never something that drew me the same way it draws some of my friends.

I'm starting to understand now.

"Tilt your head back."

"Ramanu, you don't have to do this." Lenora gives a rough laugh. "In fact, I think now's a great time to suck your cock. Or skip straight to the pegging."

I sink my fingers into her hair and tighten my hold just enough to keep her on her feet. "If you won't allow me to help you elsewhere, you *will* allow me to have my way here, little witch. You said you want a distraction, then I'll give you one. On my terms."

Her breathing goes a little rough. "And if I tell you to fuck off?"

"Don't." I'll respect her wishes, even if it kills me to do so, but I desperately don't want her to call my bluff.

Finally, Lenora curses. "Have it your way. I'll play docile little doll for you, Ramanu. For now." She tilts her head back until it's resting against my palm. "Better?"

"Much." I don't care if she's being snarky. She's giving me what I want, what I need, and that's enough. I hope I can give her some of what she needs in turn.

After she wets her hair, I work shampoo carefully into the length. It soothes me in a way I'm not entirely prepared for. Even better is the way the tension leaks out of Lenora's body until she's leaning against me, her forehead to my chest.

I guide her to rinse it, taking my time, and then repeat the process with conditioner. This time, when I rinse, I work my hand down to the base of her skull and the tight knots of tension there. She moans a little, and her hands come up to grip my sides. "Why are you trying to seduce me? I'm a sure thing."

I snort. "Nothing about you is a sure thing, little witch."

"That's not true." Her words are slow, but her energy looks good. The red is gone, taking the pale blue and gray with it. Now there's only pink and the deep blue of contentment. And *I'm* the one who put it there.

"It is." I reach past her and turn the shower off. "Let's finish this on the bed."

"Finally." But the word has no barbs, and she only mutters a little when I pluck the towel out of her hands and slowly dry her body. "Pegging."

"I'm not finished yet."

I lay her out facedown and find some conveniently stashed lotion on the dresser. Yeah, I'm really starting to see the potential of this care and pampering of one's person. I like this. A lot.

I kneel over her and focus on working every bit of tension out of her body. I inhale the little sounds she makes when I work a particularly intense knot in her shoulder. Desire is a weight against my skin, but this isn't about me. This is about giving her whatever reprieve she'll allow.

Words bubble up inside me, reassurances and promises that Lenora won't accept. I lock it all down. She *will* accept pleasure...and so pleasure is what I'll give.

CHAPTER 11

LENORA

Ramanu isn't using any magic, but they weave a spell around me all the same. They work their way down my back and gently drag their claws over my ass then start on my legs. I'm both relaxed and so turned on that I'm shaking. I never want this to stop, but if they don't *touch* me soon, I might die.

"*Ramanu.*"

"Yes, little witch?" They dig their thumb into the arch of one foot. "Do you need something?"

The demon is such a tease. I like it. I like that this isn't another battle of wills. They could use the chemistry between us to convince me to see things their way. I might take a strong stance verbally, but the truth is I'm terrified they're right. That my magic will give out when I need it most.

The tournament is mostly fought with magic. Some of that magic is like Skye's shifter powers, meaning it's more physical in nature, but that doesn't change the fact that a magicless person in the ring is as good as dead. Even without the amulet, Kristoff is incredibly powerful. I'm not sure I can beat him in a fair fight.

"Lenora." Ramanu trails their claws up my inner thigh. "You're tensing up and undoing all my hard work."

"Sorry," I murmur.

They pause, and I can't help tensing further, certain they're about to relaunch their argument. I can't believe they guessed the true purpose of the amulet...but I can't afford to think too closely about that, or fear may leech away the last of my strength.

If Ramanu competes...

If they take the amulet from Kristoff...

They won't even need me. They'll have access to the well of power that's kept my family afloat for more generations than I can readily count. If they're smart—and they show every evidence of being smart—they will take the amulet and leave me high and dry. What's a bargain with a human compared to celestial power?

"Do you want me to stop?"

I jolt. Ramanu is doing their best to give me what I asked for, and I'm still managing to ruin it. I push to my hands and knees, and they move back to allow me to face them. This is the moment to halt things once and for all, to banish them and face the mess I made with my carelessness on my own. No one forced me to fuck Kristoff and then trust him enough to fall asleep in his bed. No one else should have to bear the burden of retrieving what I lost.

I stroke my fingers over Ramanu's jaw. "You won't change my mind."

"I'm starting to see that." They don't sound happy about it. "Don't send me away."

I can almost believe they mean that because they aren't ready to stop spending time with me. It hurts how badly I want to believe it. That deep need inside me is reason enough to send them away right here and now. It's the smart thing to do. The *safe* thing to do. Apparently I haven't learned my lesson, though, because I drag my thumb over their bottom lip. "Were you serious about the pegging?"

They smile against my thumb. "I'm always serious about pegging."

"You've taken care of me. Let me take care of you right back." I try for a smile of my own. "I have a wicked strap-on spell that I think you'll like."

They burst out laughing. "Of course you do."

"Kiss me."

They surge forward and take my mouth. They were careful last time, their attention split between me and the greater crowd. That's not the case now. Every bit of their formidable attention is focused on me. They kiss me as if all the answers lie on my tongue, if only they can coax them free.

I lean back, taking them with me, letting their weight press me against the mattress. Maybe I should feel trapped, but instead it's a comfort, as if they're keeping me from floating away entirely.

Ramanu hooks one of my knees and tugs it up so I can curl my leg around their waist. They settle more firmly into the cradle of my thighs. The massage was all the foreplay I need. I'm so wet, I'm practically dripping. I fully intend to get to the promised pegging, but...this is nice.

They kiss me like the kiss is the main event. As if they're not rushing on to the next bit. As if they don't care if we run out of time and don't get around to fucking. As if the kiss has them as drugged and devastated as it has me.

They cradle my face with one hand, tilting my jaw to deepen the kiss. Gods, it's too good. I can almost convince myself that they care, that they cherish me as much as their body is conveying. It's not the truth. This is just sex, and if it's sex with someone I actually like, that doesn't change the result.

I have no future with Ramanu.

Even if I took their deal, the power imbalance between us would always sway in their favor. We would never stand on equal ground, and no matter how much they seem to value me, that is something I *need*.

I want a partner. A full partner. I don't know if that's in the cards for me, but it certainly isn't with this demon.

The realization hurts far more than it has any right to.

They break the kiss and ease back just enough to say, "Stop that."

I can't even pretend I don't know what they're talking about. Even as distracted as they are with kissing me, surely they can see the mess my emotions are right now. "What color is lust?"

For a moment, I think they won't engage, but they finally press a kiss to my jaw. "Bright pink. Neon, really." They drag their mouth down my neck. "It's pretty. Like you."

It's on the tip of my tongue to ask what color love is, but I chicken out before the words can cross my lips. It doesn't matter. There might be attraction and a thread that could become genuine caring between us, but I've known this demon less than twenty-four hours. Love isn't even in the realm of possibilities. I whimper as they set their teeth against my neck. "You're pretty, too."

"I know."

That surprises a laugh out of me. "Yeah, I guess you would. No false modesty for you."

"It's a waste of time."

I laugh again and stroke my hands down their back. I don't dig my nails in, but I love the way they shiver against me in response to the slight prick of the points. "You're right. It *is* a waste of time." I kiss their jaw, their throat, their shoulder. "Let me up. We both need this."

"Do you even know what you need, little witch?" Their voice is low and sinful in my ear. They roll their hips a little, their cock rubbing against my clit. It feels good. Really good. They nip my earlobe. "I don't think you do. So defensive. Such high walls. Such lovely spikes."

My head is spinning with pleasure, but their words feel like someone throwing rocks through my living room window. "I didn't ask for you to...*ah*." They roll their hips again—another long drag of their hard length against me. I drag in a rough breath. "This is just sex."

"No, it's not." They shift back onto their heels. "You like me. I like you. That's more than just fucking."

They're right. I hate that they're right. I can't quite catch my breath, can't think, can't do anything but sit up to close the new distance between us. "Doesn't mean anything."

"That's a different argument altogether." They kiss me hard. "It means something to me, Lenora. *You* mean something to me."

I press my palm to their horn, a tiny prick of pain blossoming there. Maybe it's not wise to use magic for this, but they've just spent so much time taking care of me. I want to return the favor. I want them to know this means something to me, too, even if it was doomed from the start.

I speak the required words, and magic surges from my palm. It's a similar spell to the ribbons, with magic forming the harness around my hips and the attached strap-on.

Ramanu makes a sound that's almost a whimper. "What is *that?*" They drag one claw down it's bright pink length and then truly whimper when it twitches in response.

"What's the point of a magic strap if it's not *magic?*" I nudge them back and slide out from beneath them. Then I walk to the gift basket on the dresser that neither of us bothered to unpack earlier. Sure enough, there's a cute little bottle of lube nestled between a package of cookies and a coupon for a free tarot reading.

Ramanu hasn't moved from their position. I consider our options. "Do you want top or bottom?"

"Bottom."

That makes things easier and gives me more control. "On your stomach."

They obey at once. I move to straddle their hips. For all my impatience earlier, I'm not about to rush this now. It's a relief to focus on Ramanu and this moment. I'm in control. Even if that only as lasts until our next orgasm, it's enough to make the ground feel steadier beneath my feet.

I drag my nails lightly down their back and then follow the faint scratches with my mouth. Teasing them. Taking care of them. By the time I reach the small of their back, Ramanu is shaking. Gods, but I like that.

It's not enough, though. I want everything.

I move off the bed and tug on their hips until they follow me back. "Turn over."

"Lenora—"

"Let me take care of you, Ramanu. Don't make me beg."

They aren't quite as coordinated as usual. I like that. A lot. So much so that I push back my own need and repeat the process to their chest. Nails, then mouth. This time, I don't stop at their hips, though. I suck their cock into my mouth and then spend several long seconds teasing them. Licking down their length. Flicking the head with my tongue. Playing with them until their thighs shake and they're making that delicious whimpering sound.

I pause long enough to coat the strap with lube before I drag the head over their ass and then add a bit more lube for good measure. A quick thought has the strap's circumference shrinking a bit. I don't want to hurt them, and since we haven't done this before, I'm not entirely certain what they can take.

Ramanu whispers something in a language I don't under-

KATEE ROBERT

stand as I work into their ass. They fist the sheets, their body shaking with the obvious effort to remain still. I go slow, but it doesn't take long before I'm seated completely. Evne though it's my spell, I can't *feel* it the way I could if it was an actual body part of mine, but I get the shadow of pleasure and it's enough to make me bite my lip.

"How's that?"

"Good," they whisper.

"Mmm." Another thought has the strap growing inside them, just a little. "And that?"

They moan and arch their back. "Goddess, Lenora. *More.*"

I grow it in small increments, watching them closely, checking in each time. On the fourth increase, Ramanu cries out. "Perfect."

I press their legs up and back. "Hold your knees for me."

After adding a bit more lube, I fuck them slowly. It takes a few strokes to get the rhythm down, but Ramanu is so responsive, I don't have to guess what they like. I drip lube over their cock and press it to their stomach with the heel of my hand. Each stroke jerks them against my palm. "More?"

"*Yes.*"

I drag in a breath and focus. Inside them, the length starts to move.

"*Fuck.*" Ramanu shreds the sheets with their claws. "Lenora, I'm going to—"

"Do it." I pick up my pace. It's hard to hold my magic concentration and keep the rhythm smooth, but it's so worth it to watch them come apart for me. "Cum for me, Ramanu."

Their back bows and they shout my name. One stroke and then a second and they're coming, their seed lashing their stomach. I bite my bottom lip and drag my fingers through the mess. "Beautiful."

"I can't... You just..." They shake their head. "Goddess, but you're a gift."

"I know." I reduce the size of the strap and then ease carefully out of them before I mutter the words to end the spell. It takes energy to use a spell instead of a real object, but you can't beat the easy cleanup. "Just let me get—"

Ramanu moves before I can finish the sentence. They sit up and hook me around the waist, then flip us so quickly, I spend a moment wondering what the fuck happened. I stare up at them.

They grin. "Come now, little witch. You didn't think we were done, did you?"

"Actually—" I gasp as they press into me. "Impressive recovery time."

"You aren't the only one with tricks up your sleeve."

They start fucking me in long, deep strokes that curl my toes and chase what little thought I have from my mind. I can do nothing but let my body take over. The pleasure washes away my fears, my stress, my everything. There is only Ramanu and their body moving with mine. It feels good, like we're old lovers instead of barely more than strangers. They touch me as if they really do care.

I don't know what to do with that. So I don't think about it at all. I dig my nails into their ass, urging them deeper. "Harder."

Ramanu shifts back, withdrawing completely. They ignore my cry of protest and flip me onto my stomach. I stop protesting then. "Yes, this." I push back, lifting my ass into the air. "Take me like this."

"Foolish little witch." They grip my hips and thrust into me. It's almost too deep, too hard, but I don't care. This is what I need. For them to *fuck* me. To make it hard and fast and rough. For it not to feel like they cherish me.

I can't afford to get any funny ideas. Not when it comes to Ramanu, and not in general. I can't afford to forget myself.

Ramanu, damn them, divines my intention immediately. "Oh no, you don't get to do that. Not with me. Not right now." They bear me down onto the mattress, covering me with their body and sliding a hand down to stroke my clit. I'm wrapped up in them, and then they go and make it even more overwhelming by continuing to speak in that sinful tone. "I have you. I might not always have you, but I do right now. You can let go."

I dig my nails into the bedding, fighting against their hold, fighting to shove myself back onto their cock. I can't get leverage. "Gods, I hate you."

"Do you want me to stop?" A thread of amusement filters in. They withdraw a little bit and chuckle when I cry out. "Didn't think so."

"Don't stop." I'm going to regret this. I just know it. I crave what they're giving me too desperately. I know what comes with forgetting yourself with a partner. Tears and loss. Heartbreak.

Ramanu isn't giving me a choice, though.

They keep fucking me slowly, moving their fingers in time with their deep strokes. It feels like they're everywhere, rubbing against all the spots designed to send me into a frenzy. I'm reduced to a whimpering, shaking thing. As my orgasm rises in a wave designed to sweep me away, the only word I'm able to speak is their name. "*Ramanu.*"

"Give it to me." Their voice has gone strained, but they don't stop, don't lose their rhythm, don't do anything but give me exactly what I need to cum so hard, I scream. "Yes, little witch, just like that." They gentle their fingers between my thighs, easing me down a little.

They shift back, pulling my hips with them so we stay joined. Their claws dig into my skin, just a little bit, and they begin to move. Ramanu does nothing halfway, and they don't simply fuck me. No, they pick up their pace slowly, doing something with their hips that has them dragging over my G-spot with each stroke.

"Oh my *gods*. Don't stop!"

For once, they don't have a smart comment. Their breathing is just as harsh as mine, and their fingers flex on my hips, the tiny pinpricks of pain only making the pleasure building in my core all the more intense. I scrabble at the torn bedding, shredding the what's left of the sheets with my nails as I cum. "*Ramanu*."

"I like it when you say my name," they gasp. "Do it again."

Lost in my orgasm, I can do nothing but obey. The last wave ebbs, and I flop to the mattress, totally spent.

Only to realize they're still hard inside me. I turn my head to the side and open one eye. "You're doing that on purpose."

"Guilty." They don't sound the least bit sorry. They wrap me up in their arms and shift so we're lying on our sides, them still buried deep inside me. "Relax. We have time."

Not enough. Nowhere near enough.

I don't say it aloud, though. Instead, I cling to them as they tuck me tighter against their body and start to move in tiny little strokes that have pleasure sparking through me yet again. If we only have this right now, I'm in agreement with Ramanu.

I don't want to waste a moment.

CHAPTER 12

RAMANU

I let Lenora sleep as long as possible. I could say it's for her benefit—and it is—but it feels good to have her in bed with me. She sleeps the same way she moves through the world, taking up more space than one would expect. Right now she's draped over my body as if she subconsciously thinks I'll slip out when she's not paying attention.

She's right.

As loath as I am to leave her, if I knew where the damned tournament is, I would already be there and waiting to step into the ring. If I get there before her and accomplish her aims before she has a chance to get hurt...

It won't work. I don't know where the tournament is, and the Shadow Market is significantly larger than I expected. I'd still be wandering the area while Lenora risks her life.

She could die.

The thought leaves me cold. I don't like the thought of this world without the little witch in it. I don't want her hurt, but the same can be said for any human I've made a bargain with. Doing so means I'm responsible for them and their safety, and I take that seriously.

It's different with Lenora.

I don't know exactly *what's* different, but I want the time to explore it with her. I want...to stand between her and the things that make the pale blue of sorrow spiderweb through her. I want her bathed forever in sunny yellow and deep ocean blue. Happy and content.

"You're very tense for someone who spent the past couple hours fucking." Lenora nuzzles my throat in a way that makes my heart do backflips through my chest. "It'll be fine."

She keeps saying that. I keep not believing her.

I want this moment to last a little longer, to preserve the peace between us. "I didn't say this earlier, but thank you for asking about terminology during our negotiation."

She smiles against my skin. "Of course. Like I said, I'm deeply invested in you having a good time, and the last thing I want is to misgender you."

That horrible warm feeling in my chest just gets stronger. I pull her close. "I prefer they/them, but honestly I don't mind the other pronouns in the right context. My gender is..." I can't help grinning a bit. "Let's call it a coat of many colors. It shifts depending on the day and my mood and the circumstances."

"A coat...of many colors. As in Joseph from the Bible?" She lifts her head. "Ramanu, you chose that metaphor on purpose just to be chaotic, didn't you?"

"Guilty." I laugh a little. "But in all seriousness, my gender is too...mischievous...to neatly categorize or pin down. I like it that way."

"I understand." Lenora presses a quick kiss to the corner of my mouth. "Thank you. For this talk, and for everything you've done since I summoned you."

The feeling in my chest gets stronger until it feels like a small sun resides in my chest. "I wouldn't have missed this time with you for the world."

"Me, either." Lenora kisses my shoulder and sits up. "It's time." She presses her fingers to my lips when I start to protest. "I have to do this. We've argued in circles, and it's obvious there's no solution that would make you happy."

"Yes, there is. Let me fight for you."

"No," she says it gently, which is almost worse than if she'd yelled it. "I won't let you get hurt on my behalf. But if it will make you too uncomfortable to watch me fight, you don't have to come."

As if I'm letting her out of my presence.

I contemplate my options as she slips into the bathroom and gets ready. My mind spins out in a thousand directions, trying to find a way through this. The problem is most routes that leave her out of danger need her active permission, and that's one thing she won't give.

It's not as if I can blame her for that. She's still reeling from Kristoff using her trust against her, and the stakes are so much higher than I could have anticipated.

There are still no answers by the time we need to leave. Lenora is giving off so much stress, her magic snapping and snarling around her, that I get a clear picture of her from head to toe. She's given up the sexy dress, replacing it with cargo pants, a long-sleeved top made of a slick material, and hefty boots. She catches me looking and pats one of her pockets. "Spell ingredients."

Clever...but only if her opponent is someone who isn't, say, immune to spells. Even if she manages to get the amulet from Kristoff's neck, she still won't have time to prepare an offensive spell.

Worry wraps its hands around my throat and squeezes tight. "Lenora—"

"Let's go."

I still haven't found a solution by the time we've worked our way through the market and stopped at the edge of a crowd. People of all shapes and sizes mill about, all soaked in the deep red of bloodlust. They want a good show, and their energy twists and burrows through the space until it makes me dizzy. I catch a few familiar strains a short distance away. There's another bargainer demon here, though I don't recognize the feel of them beyond being able to identify one of my people. Interesting.

"It's overwhelming the first time. Hang onto me." Lenora slips her hand into mine. "Come on." She tugs me through the crowd. Even here, on the cusp of what promises to be a truly violent show, they get out of her way. She doesn't seem to notice it...but I do.

A strange sort of pride takes residence at the base of my sternum. My little witch is fearsome in the extreme. Her confidence is shaken to its core, but no one would know it by the way she cuts through people much larger than her on her way to the edge of what feels like a large circle.

"Once people put their names forward, they're announced at random. You have one minute to prepare and step into the ring, or you forfeit." She takes a shaky breath I can hear even with all the people talking and shifting around us. "One chance. Fights end when someone submits, gets propelled out of the boundary of the ring...or dies."

It's difficult to tell with all the energies and magics snapping and snarling about us, but there doesn't seem to be much space between the edge of the circle and the crowd. "Are spectators often harmed?"

"A magical barrier goes up. It breaks when one of the fighters crosses it."

Hardly a foolproof solution. If one broke the barrier right as an offensive spell was launched, it would still hit the crowd. "That's not quite an answer."

"Yes, Ramanu. Sometimes people in the crowd are harmed. Most people are smart enough to have shields up, but it's not always enough. Everyone knows the risks of coming here."

I turn to her—and freeze.

In the swarm of color and energy, Lenora is dark spot. I still get a hint of color, but it's nowhere near the strength I'm used to. "Lenora."

She sighs. "Please, Ramanu. I'm not going to change my mind, and arguing is just ruin what time we have left together."

"Cast a shield."

"I can't do that because—"

"*Cast a shield.*"

She huffs, and I hear her digging into one of her pants pockets. A few seconds later, a red shield shimmers into place...but it's thin, and even as I watch, wear spots evolve into holes big enough to stick my hand through. "Your magic is faltering."

"What? No. Not yet." She mutters a word I can't quite make out and flares a brighter red. But just like before, it dwindles immediately. "No," she whispers.

"Lenora—"

"It doesn't matter." The magic drops around her, but this time it's intentional. "I'm fighting."

If she fights as little more than a normal human, then she'll die.

The knowledge feels like someone dug their claws into my chest and started digging around. I can't let her die. I refuse. Panic flares inside me, a tsunami of feelings I have no control over. They take my mouth, my tongue, my very thoughts. "Bind me."

"*What?*"

There's a stirring on the other side of the circle as people make way for someone who's a void spot to my senses. Not like Lenora is right now. No, their shields are so tight, they aren't letting a single thing out, which means they're powerful. "Who's that?"

"The official. It will start soon." Her voice only shakes the smallest bit, but it *is* shaking. Even without seeing evidence of it, knowing she's afraid has my desperation rising in response.

"Bind me, Lenora. I will win for you, and I won't be able to disobey you. I'll bring the amulet back."

"I don't believe in binding another being."

I might laugh if I didn't want to curse. "But you're fine with murder."

"It's different and you know it."

I do. I truly do. But I don't care right now. I take a deep breath and use my claw to carve the mark into the inside of my bicep. It's not one I've ever had cause to use before, but I learned early that knowledge is power, which means learning the various marks bargainer demons use with their humans... and which can be turned on us.

"Ramanu, what are you doing? Stop!"

"Cut your palm and press it to the mark. Say, 'I bind you, Ramanu.'" When she keeps sputtering, I lean down until our faces are even. "I will not let you die, Lenora. Don't ask me to stand by and allow it to happen."

She curses. "I'm releasing you the second the tournament is over. And you'd better not get hurt, or I'm going to whoop your ass." She smacks her hand against the point of my horn and then presses her bleeding palm to the mark. "I bind you, Ramanu."

The effect is instantaneous. Lenora blazes bright in front of me, as if someone shone a spotlight on her from over my shoulder. She really is beautiful, my witch. She drops her hand, looking sick. "Come back to me. Safely. Please."

It's not really a command, but the magic of the binding wraps around me and presses close all the same. "I will."

Behind me, a multitone voice cuts through the chaos of

the crowd. "The tournament will begin shortly. To put your name forward, simply raise your hand."

I lift my hand and almost immediately feel a light telepathic touch. It takes my name and little else. Around me, quiet falls aside from the shift of others raising their hands. I can't detect Kristoff; there are too many people here to pick him out after only meeting him once. If he's not here, this will all be for nothing.

The multitone voice speaks again, seeming to come from everywhere and nowhere. "Now we begin." There's no discussion of the rules or the stakes. I can appreciate that, at least in different circumstances. They call out two names, and then it's time to begin.

The first fight is between a shifter and a witch, and it's over almost before it begins. The witch casts a nasty little spell that turns the top half of the werewolf's body around like a top. I hear their spine snap from here. "Is that what you did to Skye?"

"I wasn't quite so...showy," Lenora murmurs. All her focus is on the ring as two more people are called and then two more. Some of the fights last a very long time; some, only seconds.

In the most recent fight, the loser had to be carried from the ring. Later, I'll be impressed that Lenora won this bloody, violent tournament on her own at only nineteen. Right now, I'm too damned relieved that I'm competing in her place.

"Ramanu and Charlie."

I start to step into the ring but stop when Lenora grabs my hand. She squeezes it hard. "*Win*. No matter what it takes. Come back to me."

The power of the command sizzles through me. I had already planned on doing exactly that, but it's still disconcerting in the extreme to have magic enforcing her words.

I enter the ring and take stock of my opponent. They're a

large demon, but not one from my realm. Unfamiliar isn't good, but I didn't get to where I am simply by politicking and running my mouth. The bargainer territory might have changed under Azazel's rule, but he wasn't in charge when I was born, and my parents wanted to ensure I survived *her* court. I haven't let that skill set fade since. I'm not as big as other bargainers, though, so my skills depend on my speed and agility. That will serve me here against spellcasters.

Best to get this over quickly and conserve my energy. Kristoff won't be an easy opponent.

The fight begins unceremoniously. The demon charges me, head down and arms spread. They obviously intend to wrap me in a bear hug and break me like a twig. The ring isn't big enough to dodge to either side, and I don't have time to be fancy. Their superior height works in my favor.

At the last moment, I duck out of the way then surge up, impaling them on my horns. I grab their thighs and use their speed as leverage to toss them over my head and into the barrier. It breaks with a shattering sound, and they fly into the crowd.

"Ramanu wins."

CHAPTER 13

LENORA

The fight is over so quickly, I'm still trying to process what happened when Ramanu returns to me. There's blood dripping down their horns, but they don't seem to notice it. They simply slide their hand into mine and turn to face the circle.

Three fights later and I haven't figured out what to say. Kristoff hasn't stepped into the ring yet, but as the winner from last year, he'll be seeded in the second round. "Ramanu, I—"

"Trust me."

Ironic that *they're* telling me to trust *them* when they just bound themself to me. My magic might be flickering like candlelight in a storm, but I can feel the bond between us, a live wire of dangerous possibility. Ramanu is smart and savvy and has lived far too long to give me this power. It's so easily abused. There's absolutely no guarantee that I'll hand it back once they've retrieved the amulet for me.

Kristoff wouldn't.

Many of the witches I know would give their right arm to have a demon bound to them. It's power beyond what most humans can imagine, and if it means being unscrupulous on a level even I don't dally in, there are plenty who wouldn't blink at the moral implications.

Ramanu...trusts me.

I haven't done a single thing to encourage that trust, and yet they've put their life and power in my hands. They haven't even asked for anything in return, didn't bargain and whittle away at the power I can command through them. They simply handed it over.

My throat feels thick. I can't quite swallow. This is... I don't...

"It will be okay."

"You shouldn't be the one comforting *me*." The feeling in my throat gets worse. "I won't hold the binding. I'll re—"

Ramanu presses their fingers to my lips. "Not yet, little witch. Not until I've won."

"But—"

"Ramanu and Kristoff," the announcer booms. No one really knows who they are or *what* they are; they simply show up at the Shadow Market every year and then disappear as if they never existed. They're tall, well over seven feet, and their ragged robes hang off inhumanly narrow shoulders. The robes themselves were probably black at some point but have faded to a dim gray with the ravages of time. Jack laughingly calls them the Grim Reaper, but the joke has never been funny to me.

I'm not entirely sure they're wrong.

Ramanu steps away from me, dropping my hand at the last moment before they reach the ring. Panic flutters in my chest. "Come back to me, demon."

They shoot me a fierce smile over their shoulder. "I plan on it, little witch."

I can't breathe. Gods, why can't I breathe? It's not the press of the crowd; they might be shoulder to shoulder everywhere else, but there's a circle of empty space around me. Not a large one, but there's plenty of room to inhale and exhale. Or there should be.

Instead, it's everything I can do to plant my feet and watch as Ramanu and Kristoff circle each other in the ring. Ramanu's taking a similar tactic to last time, waiting for their opponent to make the first move. Kristoff is too smart to charge in, especially considering how Ramanu's previous battle went. I don't like the look on his face, though, his smirk firmly in place and eyes mocking.

It's strange that he hasn't said a word. Normally he likes to mock his opponents into making a mistake. Maybe he knows it won't work with Ramanu?

Gods, I hope it won't work with Ramanu.

Kristoff tenses the tiniest bit. It's the only warning before he fires off a spell to incinerate Ramanu where they stand. Or it would if they were still there. They move, faster than I've seen so far, dodging the fireball with a grace that has my heart in my throat. The spell hits the boundary and shatters, causing some people in the crowd to gasp.

But Ramanu hasn't stopped moving. They come at Kristoff from the side, delivering a flurry of blows that bounce off the shield he somehow got up in time. I press my hands to my mouth, as if that's enough to keep my cry internal. "Get some distance, Ramanu." The second Kristoff finds his feet, he'll strike, and Ramanu is too close to dodge.

Except...Kristoff doesn't find his feet.

Ramanu doesn't give him a chance to. They strike and strike and strike. Their punches and kicks never touch Kristoff himself, but by hammering the shield, they drive him back toward the boundary. He's not being hurt, but he flinches every time Ramanu's fist flies at his face. My ex is more used to dueling with spells than full-out fist fighting, and it shows.

But...if he hits the boundary, this ends.

Ramanu hooks a foot around the shield a step before Kristoff crosses the boundary and sends him spinning back toward the middle of the ring. The crowd has gotten over their shock from the fireball, and they're starting to cheer my demon on.

How long can Ramanu keep this up?

I watch closely, my chest too tight and head swimming with fear, but they never falter. They never slow down. They just keep hammering at Kristoff's shield as if they can do it until the end of time... Or until the shield shatters.

Even as the thought crosses my mind, it flickers under a particularly devastating kick. Kristoff's eyes go wide, and he starts digging through his pockets, no doubt looking for a spell component that will get Ramanu off him.

He never gets a chance.

Ramanu kicks again, and this time the shield disintegrates. The blow takes Kristoff in the leg, sending him down to one knee. They don't hesitate; if anything, their speed increases. I don't even see the strike. One minute Kristoff is scrambling for a spell, and the next...my ex's head bounces across the ring.

Holy shit, Ramanu beheaded him in a single strike?

My brain can't seem to process it. The crowd has gone perfectly silent with shock. A beat. Two. On the third, someone starts cheering, and it sweeps through the space, gaining momentum and volume, until it's a roar in the throats of everyone around me.

I watch numbly as Ramanu bends down and scoops up the amulet from Kristoff's body. They walk slowly in my direction and stop a few feet away. Blood stains the links of the chain, which would horrify a normal person, but I'm still catching up.

They did it. They really did it.

They beat Kristoff.

They're safe.

My knees choose that moment to give out. I start to slump, but Ramanu does another of those too-fast moments and catches me around my waist. "Lenora?"

"I'm okay," I manage. Relief has turned my thoughts to mud. There are words I should be saying, something to reassure them, but I can't do anything except stare up into their pretty face. "*You're* okay."

"I told you I'd come back."

Distantly, I can hear Ramanu being declared the winner of the fight. There's a slight pause while someone is called to clean up Kristoff's body. I swallow hard. "You killed him."

"I'm sorry." They carefully set me back on my feet. "I know you wanted to."

I had, but how can I complain after everything that's happened? They trusted me. They fought to keep me safe. They brought my amulet back to me. I look to where it dangles from their fist. It would be the simplest thing in the world to command them to return it to me, but that feels like throwing their trust back in their face.

They start to pass it over, but I wrap my fist around theirs. "A bargain."

Ramanu goes perfectly still. "You don't have to."

"I know." But how can I repay their trust with anything but trust of my own? Someone incredibly paranoid might argue that I'm playing right into Ramanu's hands, but there's no way they bound themselves to me simply to get me to bargain. "I don't know if we have a future, Ramanu. I've only known you a short time." I take a deep breath. "But I want to give us a chance to figure it out."

"Lenora—"

Even now, they're trying to give me an out. That, more than anything, has me pushing forward. "I'll give you seven years in return for my amulet."

They hesitate. "Are you sure?"

I'm slightly terrified, but I'm sure. I haven't always made the best choices when it comes to partners, but Ramanu has shown every evidence of being kind and caring. And snarky and a little murderous, but I wouldn't have it any other way. Can't have either of us getting bored, can we? "Seven years," I repeat. "Time enough to figure out if we have something worth pursuing in a permanent way."

They smile, and it lights up their face. "Time enough, indeed." They slip their hand into mine. "Very well. Let's go collect your things and, if by the time the adrenaline has worn off, you still want to sign the contract, then we'll do it."

It's too soon for something as reckless as love, but in this moment, I know I can love Ramanu. The foundation is already there. We could have something...really special. Something like my fathers have. Something that has the potential to stand the test of time.

Neither of us speaks as we walk back to the inn. No one comments on the blood spattering Ramanu's body, but that's just the Shadow Market. A little blood is a normal occurrence, especially in this part of the market.

Ramanu excuses themselves for a few minutes once we reach the room. They return from the bathroom cleaned up and with a towel wrapped around the amulet. "You don't have to do this."

"Some bargainer demon you are." I smile a little. "You keep trying to talk me out of making a bargain with you." Every time they do, it just makes me surer that this is the right call.

Ramanu sinks onto the bed next to me and drums their fingers on their knee. Finally, they say, "A counterproposal."

It's on the tip of my tongue to tell them to stop stalling and get out the contract, but if this situation feels half as fraught to them as it does to me, it's right to talk our way through it. I swallow hard. "I'm listening."

"You keep the binding in place."

"What?" I jerk back. "No. I'm not keeping you bound. It was only for the tournament, and even then I didn't really feel good about it."

"I know." They cover my hand with theirs. "But it keeps us on equal ground, and if we want to truly see if this is worth pursuing in a permanent way, then equal ground is important."

What they're saying makes sense, but I don't like it. "That's great in theory, but we don't have the fail-safes built into the binding the same way we do into the contract. What if we fight and I accidentally command you?" I shake my head, hard. "No. It's wrong."

Ramanu considers this for several long moments. "I want you to feel good about this." They squeeze my hand. "We'll add a clause into the contract. Hold on."

Two beats later, the contract appears in the space between us. I skim it, finding it identical to what I read over before, but as promised there's a new clause near the bottom. I frown as I read it and then read it again. "It says I can't command you to commit harm against yourself."

"Yes."

"That's too narrow a restriction."

They laugh softly. "You're the only human I know who argues to have yourself *more* bound up by legalese."

"I want us on even ground." I close my eyes and think hard. "No commands, Ramanu. Not outside of a life-or-death event."

"That's too confined." They push to their feet. "You're overcorrecting."

Maybe, but I don't think so. I tap the contract. "Nowhere in here can you compel me to do anything I don't want to do. *Even ground.*"

They curse. "You're being difficult."

"And you're being stubborn." I grin. This conversation is so fraught, but I'm enjoying myself despite it. Maybe because of it, because we feel so well matched, both of us trying to look out for the other. "This is a reasonable ask."

"Fine, little witch. You win." They sink back onto the bed, and the paragraph about the binding shimmers, the words changing to reflect what we negotiated. A little thrill goes through me. We're really doing this. "Do you have a pen?"

They produce one from...somewhere. "We both sign."

That's not the normal way bargainer contracts work, but nothing about this is the normal way bargainer contracts work. "Okay." I sign my name in a quick flourish, and they do the same on the second signature line that appeared at the bottom of the contract.

The moment Ramanu lifts the pen, something sizzles in my chest. It's similar to the binding but different at the same time. I rub my sternum. "It's done."

"Yes." They take a deep breath. "Your amulet."

I lean forward so Ramanu can drape the chain over my neck. The moment it settles into place, it feels like the world shifts an inch to the right, settling back into place around me. I'd barely noticed the difference, but now I can't believe I went weeks with this vague sense of *wrongness*. I exhale slowly. "Thank you."

"Thank you for trusting me." They hesitate. "If there's anything you need to take care of before we leave, now's the time to do it. You won't be able to return for the duration."

The sheer gravity of the situation washes over me, but I chose this, and I don't regret the choice. "You said I'll be gone anywhere from a few hours to a month."

"Yes." They shrug. "It's not an exact science, but it shouldn't be longer than that."

"Okay." I take my phone and type out a quick text to Jack letting them know I'm going to be MIA for a bit. They'll have heard about the fight between Ramanu and Kristoff by now. I almost call my fathers, but it's out of character and might make them worry. Instead, I shoot a text to our family group chat and tell them I met someone and might be out of contact for a few weeks but that I'm safe and I love them. I shut off my phone and turn to Ramanu. "I'm ready."

They hold out their hand. "Let me show you my world, little witch."

I slip my hand into theirs, and everything goes black.

EPILOGUE

LENORA

S *even years later*

"IT'S TIME, LITTLE WITCH."

"Five more minutes." I stretch out in the bed I share with Ramanu, intentionally draping myself over their body in a way that makes it impossible for them to get up without displacing me. It's become a bit of a ritual between us. Sometimes they're content to let me sleep and cuddle for longer. Sometimes they really do have to go because of some responsibility to Azazel.

And sometimes we greet the morning properly.

With orgasms.

Today isn't just any other day, though. It's the seven-year anniversary of the contract we signed. When I woke up in the demon realm, lying on a fainting couch, Ramanu's fingers laced with mine, seven years felt overwhelming.

In the end, I've found a home. Not the same as my realm —not by a long shot—but a kind of home nonetheless.

I love the bargainer demon castle that shifts and changes depending on its mood. I'm still convinced it's sentient in some way, but Ramanu claims it's a spell cast by some long-dead ruler of the territory. I've made friends among the bargainer demons and in the other territories Ramanu has taken me to—dragon, kraken, gargoyle, and incubus and succubus. The relatively fraught political situation from when I arrived has morphed into what promises to be a lasting peace.

Because, in no small part, of Ramanu's interference with the various territory leaders.

I've helped, too, if I do say so myself. My old midwifery skills are no longer dusty—that much is for sure. I nuzzle Ramanu's throat. "Hey."

"Hey." They pull me closer, wrapping me up tight in their arms. "How are you feeling?"

A simple question without a simple answer. It would be easy to make a joke here, but today is the day we go beyond a test run and into a proper future. I open my eyes and lift my head. "I love you."

Their smile feels like being bathed in midsummer sunlight. "I love you, too, little witch."

I press a quick kiss to their lips. "Then I think it's time for you to meet my fathers."

"We have a few things to take care of first." They sit up, taking me with them, and scoot back so we're propped against the bed frame. Ramanu taps my chest, right over my heart. "The contract is fulfilled. Payment is accepted."

A little shiver goes through me. Most of the time, I forget about the contract entirely. It's simply never come into play. I certainly haven't been harmed...except for that business with Eve and Azazel, but it was hardly their fault that I fell, even if Ramanu acted like the pair stabbed me with a sword. It was a twisted ankle, and I was magically healed within a day, but it gave Ramanu an excuse to play nursemaid, and they seemed to enjoy that immensely.

So much so that we tried it again later in significantly sexier circumstances.

I touch my sternum, but my skin doesn't look any different. It seems wrong. After seven years and such big changes, there should be some marker. I don't look any different, though. As promised, the magic in this realm seems to have slowed my aging noticeably. "I think I'd like a mark."

Ramanu relaxes back and props their head in their hands. "You have a mark. Two, in fact."

It turns out bargainer demons have quite a few tricks up their sleeves, including tattoos that act as translation spells for both oral and written communication. A nifty trick, and I won't lie: I like having Ramanu's marks on my body in a permanent way. It also opens some *really interesting* possibilities about ancient texts back in my realm. I don't know if the spell will work with them or if it's just confined to the languages in this realm, but I'm eager to test it out.

Not yet, though.

"I want another one." I reach up and press the pad of my thumb to one of their sharp horns. The quick flare of pain makes me inhale sharply. Ramanu frowns—they don't like it when I hurt myself, even if they *do* like the results more often than not—but they don't move as I drag my thumb over the binding mark. "I release you, Ramanu." The blood smear seems to sink into their skin, marring the mark permanently. I tap it gently. "I want this."

Their frown deepens. "You want a demon-binding mark."

"No, I want *this* mark. Binding and broken. A choice." Maybe a strange choice, but one I'm making. Ramanu and I haven't really talked about marriage. At this point, it seems like a step we'd take solely for the sake of taking it, not because it marks any kind of intent. We've chosen each other. A ring or ritual won't make a difference when it's a choice we make every single day.

Granted, my fathers might have some thoughts on that, but we'll cross that bridge when we get to it.

Ramanu considers me for a long moment and finally nods. "Now?"

I nod. "Now. You're wearing my mark. I want to wear yours, too."

"Matching tattoos." They smirk. "We are a cliché."

I laugh. "Well, we're simply too unique in every other way. We're entitled to be a little cliché now and again." When they still don't move, I sit up on my knees. "Ramanu, don't tell me you're afraid of that silly human superstition that getting matching tattoos heralds the end of a relationship."

They open their mouth, seem to reconsider, and close it. "Not afraid. Perhaps a bit superstitious."

"I choose you," I say softly. "I'm going to keep choosing you. This won't always be easy. There will be times I'm definitely tempted to hex you and you'll definitely want to toss me into a portal to another realm, but..." We don't always get mushy with our words, yet it feels right in this moment. "I've never had a relationship last as long as this one, and it's not just because of the binding and the contract. I *trust* you. I have fun with you. I feel safe enough to talk my way through any shit that pops up. I love you, Ramanu. Getting a tattoo isn't going to change any of that."

They cup my face with a clawed hand. "You know I feel the same way, little witch. These past seven years haven't always been easy, but I wouldn't have it any other way. You're it for me."

"You're it for me, too."

They nod slowly. "Very well."

It takes no time at all for them to ink the mark into my

skin with their blood—the bargainer demons' preferred method when it comes to marks because of their magic—and then carefully mar it with a streak the same way I did. It hurts but that feels right.

Nothing worth having comes without sacrifice, and the pain is a small price to pay for the meaning behind this, the trust we're continuing to place in each other.

Ramanu kisses me. "I love you."

"I love you, too." Maybe I'm a sap, but I never get tired of hearing or saying that. Every time the words cross their lips, Ramanu has an almost marveling tone. I keep waiting for it to ease, for us to settle into expecting love instead of being bliss-fully happy to have it, but it hasn't happened yet.

"Explaining this to my fathers is going to be...something."

They grin. "Do I have to worry about shotguns?"

"No, nothing like that." I roll my eyes. "But Dad had some strong feelings about his grandmother and her, ah, infatuation with you. I'm sure he's going to have equally strong feelings about the fact that we're together."

Ramanu gives a delicate shudder. "I wish you wouldn't bring her up. She was a terrifying human—far too terrifying for my tastes. You're the only one who's enticed me enough to break the rules."

"I'm special like that." As tempting as it is to stay in bed and prolong this moment of peace, our seven years are up. Azazel has promised I'm free to come and go with Ramanu between realms, but there's still *my* family to deal with. My fathers will have reservations about Ramanu, but we have time to win them over.

We have the rest of our lives.

We take our time getting ready and packing up the few things I refuse to travel without. Ramanu dresses in one of their best outfits, one nearly identical to what they wore when

I initially summoned them all that time ago. I grin. "Looking to make a good impression?"

"Your fathers matter to you." They point at me. "And don't pretend like you weren't about to vomit out of sheer nerves when you met my parents."

I shudder. "I don't have any idea what you're talking about. I wasn't nervous at all." Lies. I get along well enough with Ramanu's parents now, but there was a lot of reserve on all sides initially. Ramanu did break the rules with me, after all. Their mother was pretty pissed about that, even if their parent found it amusing to see their child so twisted up over a cute little human. Their words, not mine.

We walk together through the shifting halls of the castle to Azazel's office. It's in a different location every time, and I have the distinct suspicion he uses it to hide from his people from time to time. Being the leader of an entire territory seems like a headache.

He looks up when we walk through the door. Azazel shares Ramanu's crimson skin and black claws and horns—though he's only got one set—but he's a bit bigger all around. Honestly, he looks kind of like what the Christian devil is supposed to be like, which I've always found privately hilarious. Not even I would say as much to his face.

He scans us. "You're ready."

"Yes." Ramanu shifts a little closer to me until our shoulders touch. "I don't know how long I'll be gone, but plan for it to be longer than expected."

"We can hold down the fort without you for a bit. Go. You've worked hard to get where you are, Ramanu. There's no shame in taking time for yourself and those you love." Azazel smiles. He looks fearsome as fuck, but I learned a long time ago that he's a big softie. It's cute to watch him with his humans, though he wouldn't thank me for pointing that out, either.

He turns his attention back to me. "Lenora, as previously discussed, you're always welcome here. Ramanu has blanket permission to bring you over whenever they like."

That took a wicked little bit of magic to pull off, since most humans need bargains to travel between realms. I've learned a lot by being here. I grin. "Thanks. I will continue to be a giant pain in your ass."

"I expect nothing less."

Ramanu slips their hand into mine. "Let's go, little witch."

"After you, demon." I grin. I never could have anticipated this being my life, but I wouldn't have it any other way.

THANK you so much for reading *The Demon's Bargain*! If you enjoyed the story, please consider leaving a review.

BONUS EPILOGUE

AN EROTIC SHOW

" **I** have a surprise for you."

I'm already grinning as I turn to face Ramanu. If all our years together have taught me anything, it's that when they have something up their sleeve, it's going to be a rollicking good time. "Tell me."

"Then it wouldn't be a surprise." They hold out their hand. "Come on. I have some clothing set out for you. We wouldn't want to stand out too much for this little trip."

Curiosity sinks its fangs into me and I slip my hand into theirs. "What brought this on?"

"Do I need a reason to surprise you with things?"

I roll my eyes. "No, of course not, but it's not an anniversary and it's not a birthday or even a holiday. Normally you have a reason for springing this kind of thing on me."

"I'm running a little errand for Azazel." They tug me behind them down the hall of the castle toward our room. Or, rather, the castle shifts to deliver us to our room. Even a decade later, I'm not entirely certain if this place is sentient or not, but I still pat the doorframe in thanks as I pass through.

Never hurts to be polite.

When Azazel and Eve were fighting during those early days, the castle tended to spit him out in the dungeons, the canal, even into the sewers on one particularly memorable occasion. Best to avoid pissing off a magical building who can be petty like that.

Azazel has laid out a pretty gown on our bed. It's the deepest crimson and when I strip and pull it over my head, I find that there's a slit on either side that goes up to the top of my hip. It reminds me of the dress I wore that first Samhain, just a little bit. "Easy access."

"That's the idea. Turn."

I obey and they lace up the bodice. "So when are you telling me where we're headed?"

"When we get there." They duck into the closet and emerge a few moments later a garment that's a cross between a kilt and a skirt, just as black as mine. They have, however, forgone any shirt at all.

I lift my brow. "Are we attending a funeral?"

"No, we're making a statement." They offer their elbow. "Come on. We don't want to be late."

Late for *what?*

I already know they won't answer if I keep asking, so the only way to find out is to take their arm and let them teleport me to our destination. It's not any easier on my stomach than it was the first few times. The human body simply is not made to jump time and space the way a bargainer demon can.

We've found our workarounds, though. Ramanu hands me the little vial as soon as we land, and I down it as quickly as possible, clamping my jaws together in an effort to keep my stomach from rebelling. "I hate this."

"Hate the process, love the results." They wrap an arm around my waist. "Come on."

I straighten...and pause. We've done a bit of realm-jumping in the time we've been together; enough to know we're not in the human realm here. The buildings are all wrong, a vaguely familiar older style but without the age that marks all of their kind in my realm. More, the people walking the streets are just as varied as we find in the Shadow Market. "Where are we?"

"Secret." They grin, a flash of teeth and mirth. "But this isn't the surprise."

I inhale deeply. "Do I smell the sea?"

"Mmm."

I tug playfully on their arm. "You're being so secretive. Can we explore this place after we do whatever you've brought me here to do?"

"Of course. We have as much time here as we'd like. The monarch and I have an understanding, and Azazel's errand doesn't require a rush."

If anything my brows rise higher. "Ramanu—"

"If we don't hurry, we're going to miss the opening act."

I do my best not to gawk at the square as Ramanu tows me across it, though I can't help eyeing the stocks that occupy the middle of the space. They look....well-used.

Our destination is a tall brown building with pretty stained glass windows. Ramanu holds open the door for me and I have to pause just inside to let my eyes adjust to the dim lighting. The inside is set up like a theater with raised levels on either side and a scattering of tables on the floor before the stage. The whole space is filled with a variety of people, an equal mix of human and blatantly magical beings. The light of the setting sun paints the stage in a riot of color. "We're seeing a show?"

"Mmmm."

Ramanu leads me to the stairs and up to the second level. It's been sectioned off so we have privacy but can see the stage clearly. My curiosity has reached boiling point. Ramanu likes their secrets and surprises, but they're playing particularly coy this time.

It means this is going to be good.

The lights dim, except for the stained glass sunbeam on the stage. Ramanu pulls my chair close and murmurs in my ear. "Their sunset show is one of their best."

I don't see much of the rigging or that sort of thing that a normal theater employs to put on a show and transport an audience to another place. What *is* this?

The answer comes as a woman dances out onto the stage. She's short and white with long dark hair and has the same body type most ballerinas do. She's dressed in a short red dress that spins about her body, showing off lace panties in a matching color. Even from this distance, I can see the shadow of her pussy.

Normal ballerinas don't wear *that* on stage.

I look at Ramanu in question, but they're watching me. "Pay attention, little witch. You're not going to want to miss this."

As the woman spins and twirls, I belatedly realize that the stained glass has painted a maze onto the floor of the stage. Anticipation curls through me. I do love a good maze.

When she reaches the center, she spins and spins and spins. I'm so busy watching her hypnotic movement that I almost miss she's no longer alone on the stage.

The minotaur that rises from the center of the maze through a clever circular contraption is tall, much taller than Ramanu and *significantly* taller than the little ballerina. He's also wearing only a loincloth and it does nothing to hide that he's aroused.

I lean forward in anticipation as he circles the woman. He doesn't touch her, doesn't close the distance between them, but even from this distance, I'm nearly certain his cock gets harder.

I'm so caught up in them that I actually gasp when she stops spinning and faces him. Their size difference is so pronounced, it makes my pussy pulse.

"I knew you'd enjoy this," Ramanu murmurs. "Come here, little witch."

I don't take my eyes from the stage as I slip my hand into theirs and allow them to guide me to sit on their lap. They run their claws lightly over my bare thighs. Teasing, but not enough to distract me from the show itself.

The minotaur and the woman circle each other, each movement a perfect mirror for the others. Their dance is a seduction, and even as I hold me breath, waiting for the moment when they'll touch, I want it to last forever.

It doesn't, of course.

The minotaur catches the edge of the ballerina's dress as she spins away, and it comes off her in ribbons. She reaches the edge of the center of the maze wearing only her shoes and her panties. She makes a half-hearted attempt to cover her small, perfect breasts, but it looks more teasing than shy.

The music changes.

I almost don't notice Ramanu slipping their hand beneath my dress. They brush my pussy with their knuckles as the minotaur stalks the woman out of the center of the maze and through its winding paths. Her movements are both frightened and also teasing; a combination I'm not sure how she pulls off.

I lean back against Ramanu's chest and trace my fingers along their forearm. They take that as invitation to press two fingers into me. My gasp is swallowed by the crowd as the minotaur catches the ballerina.

He's so much bigger than her that his hands completely encompass her waist as he lifts her high in the air. She shakes her head in protest, but she braces her knees on his shoulders so he can get to her pussy with his mouth.

Her hips roll as his long tongue works her through her panties.

"Oh wow."

"Do you like the game of protest?" Ramanu's voice in my ear as their lips brush the sensitive spot behind it.

"Do you?"

"Yes." They smile against my skin. "I like both sides of it."

The possibilities stretch out before me as the minotaur hauls the ballerina back to the center of the maze. He lowers her, but doesn't give a chance for her feet to touch the ground.

I see where this is going and reach back to palm Ramanu's cock. "I need you inside me when he takes her."

They don't argue. They also don't take their fingers from me as we wrestle their pants down enough to free their cock. I never take my gaze from the stage. The minotaur rips off her panties and her carefully orchestrated struggles cause his loincloth to fall in the process.

"Oh my."

He's *massive*.

Ramanu notches their cock at my entrance, but they don't pull me down its length. I bite my bottom lip and watch as the minotaur flips the ballerina around so she's facing the audience and catches her thighs, spreading her wide. She's given up her faux-protest and has her arms over her head, reaching as much of his face as she can as he lowers her onto his cock.

I lower myself onto Ramanu's cock in time with the ballerina's descent. Their claws dig into my hips just a bit, a little pain to heighten the pleasure.

And there is...so much pleasure.

Both in watching and in the doing.

I am who I am, though, and it doesn't take long for me to forget myself. I brace my hands on the railing in front of me and ride Ramanu's cock, chasing the pleasure I see being enacted on the stage below.

Just like that, it's not enough to watch. I pull myself off their cock and turn around to straddle them. Their lips are parted as they moan a little. I will never get tired of seeing them like this. The game of dominance and submission is one we take turns playing, and they might have started tonight in the dominant role, but I need it now.

I grab on of their horns and push their head back so I can drag my tongue up their throat. "Do you want me to chase you, Ramanu?"

Their hands spasm at my hips, guiding me to increase my pace. "Maybe I want to chase you."

I kiss them hard and then move to whisper in their ear even as I ride them hard. "Will you run from me, demon? Let me chase you through a maze of our creation?" My pleasure is strung so tight, I'm about to cum, but I need to get this out first. This is one fantasy we haven't actually played at, and I need to see it to its conclusion. "Should I catch you with my magic, hold you down, take what you pretend you don't want to give me..."

Ramanu moans and pulls me close. "You're a *menace*."

"I'm *your* menace."

They release my hips to cup my face and kiss me. It starts out hard and messy, just enough of both to push me over the edge. I cry out against their mouth as I orgasm, and then I drink down their own moan of release as they follow me over the edge.

They never stop kissing me, though.

Distantly, I'm aware of applause as the minotaur and the ballerina finish their act. I don't have the strength to lift my head, though. I'm too wrapped up in my demon.

Ramanu is the one to gentle the kiss and ease me off them. "The show's not over yet."

I blink at them. "It's not finished."

They laugh softly. "Not by a long shot."

My heart goes soft and hot, all at the same time. "This might be your best surprise yet."

"Believe me, little witch, the feeling is entirely mutual." They arrange me against their chest as the lights change again. "Now you have me considering how best to conjure up a hedge maze. Who knows what the next decade will bring?"

"Only joy. And a lot of good sex."

They hug me tight. "I love you."

"I love you, too." I pause and frown down at the stage. "Is that a *kraken*?"

***

We hope you enjoyed Ramanu and Lenora's story! Be sure to sign up for Katee's newsletter to see what's coming next in this world!